FIREHOUSE DOG

Adapted by MICHAEL ANTHONY STEELE

Screenplay by CLAIRE-DEE LIM & MIKE WERB
& MICHAEL COLLEARY

SCHOLASTIC INC.

New York   Toronto   London   Auckland   Sydney
Mexico City   New Delhi   Hong Kong   Buenos Aires

ISBN-13: 978-0-439-89642-9
ISBN-10: 0-439-89642-8

Published by Scholastic Inc.
SCHOLASTIC and associated logos are trademarks and/or registered trademarks of Scholastic Inc.

12 11 10 9 8 7 6 5 4 3 2 1   7 8 9 10 11/0

Designed by Rick DeMonico
Printed in the U.S.A.
First printing, February 2007

1

Liz Knowles stepped over snaking electrical cables and ducked under a hot light as she marched across the movie set. Normally, on a movie of this scale, the set would be alive with activity. Crew members would buzz about, adjusting lights, placing cameras, and moving scenery. On this set, however, the entire crew sat around doing nothing. Of course, what could they do? The star of the film had refused to leave his trailer.

As she exited the studio, she strode toward the row of RVs parked along the street. She zeroed in on the biggest one, the temporary home of the biggest star she'd ever worked with. Two hulking bodyguards stood on either side of the trailer's door. As she neared, the men nodded and stepped aside. The producer climbed the steps and raised a tight fist, intending to pound on the large brass star mounted to the door. Then she paused, took a deep breath, and tucked a loose strand of her dark hair behind her ear. Liz plastered a smile on her face and gently rapped on the star. After some movement inside, the door opened slightly.

"Hey, Liz," said Trey Falcon as he peeked through the small opening. "What's up?"

"*Time* is up, Trey," she replied, trying to sound calm. "Is he coming out or not?"

Trey glanced around. "It's looking bad. He's really depressed."

Liz rolled her eyes. "Why?"

Trey frowned as he swung open the door. "Come in. But park the negativity outside."

Liz stepped into the dimly lit mobile home. Velvet cushioned couches lined the walls. Soft music filled the air along with the light scent of jasmine. An open bottle of mineral water sat on the coffee table next to a covered dish and an opened script. The star of her film was nowhere in sight.

Trey sighed. "First of all, this place is not clean enough."

"Trey." She spread her arms wide. "It's practically sterile."

"Dust allergies," Trey said, tapping his pointed nose. "How can he do high-altitude stunts when his sinuses are throbbing?" The man bent down and pulled the cover from the dish. "And this." He nodded to the large steak on the plate beneath. "This is *not* Kobe beef. Trust me, he knows the difference." He quietly replaced the lid and leaned toward Liz. "But that's nothing compared to the real problem." He glanced toward the master bedroom and carefully opened a nearby cabinet. He pulled out a small fleece sweater — white with black spots.

"A fleece?" asked Liz.

He cringed at her loud voice and quickly tossed the sweater back into the cabinet. "A Dalmatian spotted fleece. One of your production assistants was wearing it," whispered Trey.

"So what?" asked Liz.

"It reminds him of the girl who broke his heart, that's so what," he replied. "And at the moment, he can't think of anything else."

Liz couldn't believe her ears. "Trey, the director is furious. The crew has been waiting for hours. . . ." She removed her glasses and rubbed her eyes. "There must be something I can do."

Trey shrugged and smiled. Then he took Liz's hand and led her toward the closed bedroom door. Very gently, he knocked on the door and turned the knob.

Inside, the star of her movie lay on a huge hexagonal bed. At first glance, he might have looked like any other Irish terrier (albeit one wearing silk pajamas and a diamond-studded collar). However, after noticing the swooping Mohawk atop his head, anyone who hadn't been living under a rock for the past three years would recognize Rex, the world's biggest canine action star.

The dog was surrounded by triumphs of his film career. The walls were adorned with movie posters from his latest hits: *Terrier at 20,000 Feet, Jurassic*

Bark, and *The Fast and the Furriest*. Several awards and framed publicity photos were neatly arranged on the nearby dresser. Yet, despite being among his countless trophies, the dog sighed sadly.

Liz crept toward him. "Rex, I am so sorry for your loss. It's always the true artists who suffer the most."

Trey knelt beside the bed. "Alas, all he sees is that beautiful Dalmatian Lola."

Rex continued to stare blankly as Liz crouched as well. "I know it hurts — I've been dumped more times than I can count." She leaned forward. "But think of your career. Without you, there is no movie or your first percentage that goes with it."

"I tried the money thing," admitted Trey. "He didn't bite."

As Liz gazed around the room, an idea came to her. She spun back to Rex. "What about your legacy?" she asked.

Rex's ears perked. He extended a paw toward the producer.

"I had no idea," Trey muttered.

Liz gently stroked his paw. "Rex, compared

to you, that talking Chihuahua is just a footnote in history."

That did it. Rex sprang to his feet. He wagged his tail and gave a loud bark.

Trey moved to the dresser. "Let's get his costume on!" He grabbed a worn leather collar with a dangling brass tag. "Secret Agent Dewey Branson is ready for action!"

Rex panted happily as Trey removed his pajamas and diamond-studded collar. Then he replaced it with the leather one. The man gave the dog a gentle pat on the head, carefully avoiding Rex's swooping hairpiece. "Let's shoot this thing, buddy!"

The terrier barked once more and bounded off the bed. He sprinted out the door.

Trey smiled and hugged Liz. "You're a miracle worker!"

Rex steadied himself as the small plane bucked beneath his paws. They flew below darkening clouds, but there was no rain yet. The gathering storm didn't bother the dog, however. He had performed far more dangerous stunts than this. Besides, he knew the black clouds would make for a more dramatic shot.

Trey and Liz were a different story. They sat, strapped in, on the other side of the cabin. Trey checked his seat belt for the fifth time. Liz held tightly to her chair's arms. They both wore worried expressions.

"We're almost over the drop zone," said the pilot's voice from the intercom. "Two minutes."

A special-effects technician turned Rex's small parachute over in his hands, inspecting it one last time before placing it on the dog. Another tech slid open the side hatch. A rush of wind ruffled Rex's coarse coat and he wagged his tail. He was ready to get this show on the road.

CRACK!

A bolt of lightning struck the plane. Rex was temporarily blinded as light filled the tiny cabin. The plane shook and a small *POP* sounded out. The parachute opened and billowed toward him. Once again, Rex was blinded as the white silk enveloped him.

As the dog tried to shake the parachute from his face, the plane banked to the right. Rex felt himself slide across the floor. He spread his legs as his claws scraped against metal.

"Rex!" yelled Trey.

Then he was suddenly free of the parachute. He could see once more. He could see the plane above him growing smaller and smaller as he tumbled through the air — without his chute.

Trying not to panic, Rex righted himself and looked down at the rapidly approaching ground. Skydiving was never a problem for the action star.

However, skydiving without a parachute was a *huge* problem. The ground grew closer.

To make things worse, Rex's hairpiece was ripped away from his head. The dog never went anywhere without it. Of course, it wasn't as big a problem as the missing parachute. After all, he owned fifteen spare hairpieces. He just hoped the crew below wasn't filming yet.

Suddenly, he saw something familiar, a small red rectangle far below him. With dog years of experience, he tucked in all four legs and pointed his nose toward the object. It had to be a stuntman's air bag. After all, they were very close to the drop zone when he was ejected from the plane.

When he was directly over the bag, Rex spread his legs to steady his descent. The red rectangle grew larger as he sped downward. Then, at the last possible moment, the seasoned stunt dog spun his body so he would land on his back. This time, he didn't feel the familiar slap of the bag.

SPLAT!

The air bag was neither a bag nor full of air. Rex

landed in a truck full of tomatoes. The terrier clawed his way to the top. When he reached the surface, he spat out a mouthful of slimy skins and seeds. He hated tomatoes. He tried to shake off the red remnants but did little good. He was covered, from head to tail, in tomato guts.

Rex tried to scramble out of the mess, but each paw plunged deep with each step. The best he could do was make his way to the side of the truck. Before he could climb up the railing, the truck began to move. Rex was thrown back into the middle of the tomato pile. His eyes rolled and he passed out.

Liz pushed through the dense underbrush. She scanned the ground with the bright beam of her flashlight. The dark woods were full of sound as more beams of light crisscrossed in the darkness. The entire film crew turned out to look for Rex.

Haggard, Trey tromped along beside her. Then his flashlight beam stopped on something lying on the forest floor. He ran to the spot and dropped to the ground. When he rose, he held Rex's small

Mohawk hairpiece. "We're close." He picked a leaf from the tangled hair. "We have to keep looking."

Liz sighed. "His hairpiece could have landed miles from the . . . rest of him." She put a hand on Trey's shoulder. "There are lakes and rivers all over the place. . . ."

The man quivered as he clutched the hairpiece to his chest. "I was supposed to take care of him. "

Liz pulled him close as he sobbed on her shoulder. When he was ready, they continued their search. They continued long into the night.

Smoke choked the dark room as flames climbed its walls. A young boy coughed as he stumbled over the smoldering debris on the ground. He rammed his shoulder against the door and it swung outward.

"Someone . . . help me!" shouted a distant voice.

The boy shuffled into the smoke-filled corridor. Flames sprouted behind him and herded him forward and into another large room. Through a haze of smoke, the boy could just make out a thin man trapped under a large ceiling beam. "Can't . . . breathe," choked the man.

The boy ran and dropped to the floor beside him. He tried to free the man, but the beam was too heavy. He staggered to his feet and tried to run for help. Unfortunately, flames engulfed the room's only exit. The boy coughed and turned to the large window on the other side. Through the smoke-stained glass, he saw a man shuffle through the next room. He wore a thick yellow jacket, helmet, and face mask — a firefighter.

The boy ran to the window. "I'm here!" he shouted. "Dad, I'm right here!" The firefighter kept walking.

The boy reached down and grabbed an ax. With all his might, he swung the heavy tool toward the large window. The sharp blade merely bounced off the glass. Coughing louder, the boy swung again, then again. The window wouldn't break.

"No!" he yelled.

Shane Fahey woke with a start. He looked around and no longer saw smoke or flames. Instead, students sat at several tables in neat rows. He wasn't in a burning building after all. He was in the school cafeteria.

Shane gave a small cough as he wiped a few brown strands of hair from his damp forehead. Luckily, no one seemed to notice he'd fallen asleep — no one but his two friends sitting next to him. They both held food to their open mouths, staring at him.

Oscar was the first to break the silence. "Shane, you're drooling." The heavyset boy laughed and went back to his sandwich.

"Dude, you were seriously freaking out," said Josh. "What's up with you?"

Shane rubbed his eyes. "Man, I didn't sleep at all last night. Eleven straight hours of Alien Siege."

Oscar swallowed a large bite. "You are *so* lucky your old man pulls twenty-four-hour shifts."

"What level did you get to?" asked Josh.

Shane leaned back. "Thirteen. I was blazing!"

"You are such a liar," said a voice behind him. He turned to see JJ Presley holding her lunch tray. The thin girl wore her blond hair in a ponytail. "There's no level higher than nine," she said with a smirk.

"Not for you," Shane replied. "You obviously didn't find the black hole."

"Therth a block hole?" Oscar asked through a mouthful of food.

JJ shook her head. "So, if you were gaming all night . . . I guess you're not worried about the science test."

14

A sharp pain stabbed Shane's stomach. He had completely forgotten. His mind raced as he wondered if he left his science book in his locker or in his backpack. The school bell rang just as he reached for it.

"See you there," chirped the girl as she headed for the door.

Shane shook his head as he and his friends gathered their things.

"Arlo took the test first period," Josh reported. "He said it was brutal."

The three boys dumped their trays and then joined the river of students flowing out the cafeteria doors. Once in the hallway, Oscar and Josh turned right, but Shane fell back.

"I'll be right there," said Shane. "I just have to go to the bathroom."

Shane couldn't bring home another F in science. He winded through the crowd and passed the boys' restroom without a glance. As the hallway thinned of students, he opened his locker and pulled out his skateboard. One minute later, he was out the front door and on his board. He ollied over the front steps and zipped down the sidewalk. Before long, Wilson Middle School and the science test were far behind him.

He turned down Wilmer Avenue, then took a right onto Fulton. He'd cut through the warehouse district where traffic was light this time of day. It was mostly downhill and he'd have the whole street to himself.

Everything was going fine until he heard an approaching vehicle. Shane swerved to the left so the car could pass. However, instead of passing, the car pulled alongside him. And instead of being a car, it was a fire rescue truck.

"How's it going, Shane?" asked a voice he knew too well. It was Terence Kahn, a new firefighter in his dad's unit. Lionel Chase, a more seasoned firefighter, rode shotgun.

Shane shook his head. "Don't you guys have a fire to put out?" He kicked off the ground, gaining some speed. The small ambulance kept pace with him.

"We're scrounging parts for the rig," Terence replied.

"Are you ditching school again?" asked Lionel. The African American man gave him a sly smile.

Shane thought fast. "Hello?" he said sarcastically. "Holiday? It's Malcolm X's birthday."

"Malcolm X's birthday?" asked Lionel. He looked at Terence. "Is that today?"

Terence slowly nodded. "Yeah . . . Malcolm X Day. Right . . ."

Shane thought he should leave while he could. "Okay, guys. It's been real." He waved.

Lionel leaned over. "Want to hitch with us?"

"No, I'm cool," Shane replied. He leaned left, turning into a side street.

"Don't be getting yourself into any trouble today, all right?" Lionel called after him.

"Thanks, Lionel!" Shane yelled without looking back. "I already have a dad," he added as he rolled away from the truck.

4

Captain Connor Fahey leaned back in his chair and took another sip of coffee. He studied the large map on the bullpen wall. He had every street memorized and knew the location of every pushpin by heart. Yet somehow, he was missing something. Maybe staring at the map would bring all the pieces together. Unfortunately, it hadn't worked so far.

He was only mildly aware of the sounds around him. Below, the rhythmic sounds of Pep Clemente's punching bag — *thumpetha-thumpetha-thumpetha* — were broken by the occasional clank or rattle of Joe Musto getting lunch ready. Then the phone rang, pulling Connor from his daze.

"Joe! Get the phone!" Pep yelled without missing a punch on her speed bag.

"*You* get it!" Joe yelled back.

"I'm working out!" Pep countered.

"I'm making lunch!" Joe yelled louder.

"You're closer!" Pep yelled, hitting the bag faster.

"Cap!" yelled Joe. "Pep won't answer the phone!"

Connor shook his head and set down his coffee. He got to his feet and strode into the nearby dormitory. He passed two of the room's cots and grabbed the brass pole in the center of the room. He slid down and marched past Pep. Her brown ponytail shook as she hammered away at the speed bag. As he passed the mess hall, Joe was working in the adjacent kitchen. The large man dug through the back of the refrigerator.

"Since you guys are so busy . . ." Connor said as he jogged to the wooden phone booth by the wall. He snatched the phone from its cradle. "Engine fifty-five, Dogpatch Station. This is Connor. . . ." He caught himself. "Captain Fahey speaking."

"Head's up, Cap," came Lionel's voice from the receiver. "We saw Shane on Fulton Avenue."

"When?" asked Connor.

"Like, right now," replied Lionel. "Maybe thirty seconds ago."

Connor heard Terence's voice in the background. "Ask him if today is Malcolm X's birthday."

Connor Fahey rubbed his forehead. A headache was coming on. "Bring him in," he ordered. He glanced toward the refrigerator. Joe pulled out a glass dish holding an unidentifiable substance — a black and green unidentifiable substance. "And maybe pick up lunch."

5

Rex ambled along an empty sidewalk. He had no idea where he was or when he'd get his next pedicure (and he certainly needed one). His nails had already begun to wear down on the hard pavement.

As unaccustomed as he was to long treks, the dog was more than happy to walk after that disgusting truck ride. He'd woken up and was able to climb out of the truck just as it pulled up to the back of a warehouse. He'd hoped the workers would recognize him and take him back to the movie set. Instead, they seemed quite angry that he'd been in their tomato truck. It wasn't Rex's fault their truck looked like a stunt bag from five thousand feet above.

He kept moving down the empty sidewalk even

though he didn't know where he was going. Rex tucked his tail between his legs. He needed to find Trey. He needed to find Liz. He needed to at least find his agent. Unfortunately, they were nowhere to be found.

Rex paused beneath a large billboard. It depicted a happy driver splashing through a large mud puddle in a white 4x4. Amazingly, no mud appeared to soil the vehicle, the driver, or the handsome dog leaning his head out of the passenger window. That dog was Rex, his hairpiece flapping in the simulated wind. Rex remembered that photo shoot well. Then he caught his reflection in a pool of water in the gutter. A disheveled, tomato-stained terrier stared back at him. Rex quivered and turned away. Forget Trey, Liz, or his agent. He needed his stylist!

As despair washed over him, he opened his mouth to howl. Yet, before he could make a sound, a loud bark echoed across the pavement. Rex trotted forward and turned the corner. An animal control truck idled as its driver placed a small dog into a cage in the back. As the short man closed the door, Rex gave a loud bark, ordering the man to release the dog at once.

Instead of doing as he was told, the man turned to Rex and smiled. "Room for one more." He grabbed a long pole from the truck and marched toward Rex. A noose dangled from one end of the pole, the end he extended toward the dog.

Rex gulped. Bad idea. The dog spun and took off down the sidewalk. Then he darted into a nearby alley. The man's footfalls were close behind him as the dog poured on the speed. Suddenly, Rex's escape was cut off by a tall chain-link fence. Dead end with nowhere to run. Rex turned to face the animal control officer.

"All try," snickered the man as he inched closer. "And all fail."

Rex turned back to the fence. There was no way he was going to be manhandled by some common brute. Then he spied a moldering mattress propped against a Dumpster. It wasn't a springboard, but it would have to do.

Rex took a few steps back. The man was almost

on top of him. Then he darted for the Dumpster. At the last moment, the dog leapt onto the mattress, bounced, and soared into the air. He performed a stunning backflip, tumbled over the fence, then landed nimbly on the other side. The man's jaw dropped. Rex turned up his nose and whipped around. He casually sauntered away from the stunned officer.

Shane kicked harder as he heard the rescue truck turn the corner behind him. Lionel and Terence had either realized that it wasn't really Malcolm X's birthday or they had called his dad. Whichever it was, neither was good. He had to ditch the truck and make his way home. That would give him time to make up a really good story. Maybe he'd say he got food poisoning from lunch. *Naw*, he thought. *I used that one last week.*

Shane leaned left, turning into a narrow alley. There was no way the big truck could fit through. He glanced back to see them pull to a stop at the alley's entrance. Its doors opened as the two men were ready to chase him on foot.

Shane kicked harder and turned back to navigate past the Dumpsters and crates. He headed straight for a big, mangy mutt! Shane tried to stop, but it was too late. He slammed into the dog. The two tumbled down the dirty alley. When they came to a stop, the big dog sat on his chest with his panting mouth in his face. The dog let out a large belch.

"Ugh!" said Shane. "Mouth fart!"

Lionel and Terence ran up as Shane pushed the mutt off of him. He slowly sat up and rubbed one elbow.

"Look at you, man," said Lionel. "What have you got to say for yourself?"

Shane didn't reply as the two men helped him to his feet. Terence grabbed his skateboard while Lionel led him back toward the truck. Shane saw the mutt trot past the vehicle and around the corner. The dog didn't seem hurt at all. In fact, he acted as if nothing happened.

"I hate that dog," Shane muttered.

Rex padded down the sidewalk, away from the boy and the two men. He didn't want to hang around and get caught up in whatever drama that was about. He had to find his way home. And one thing was for sure — it certainly wasn't there among the dilapidated buildings surrounding him. He longed for his luxurious trailer, his Kobe steak, his sparkling mineral water. His mouth began to water just thinking about it. Then all of a sudden he heard a loud *SCREEK-SCREEEEEEEK*!

The squeaking brakes of the animal control truck snapped him out of his daydream. The nose of the vehicle poked out from between two buildings ahead. Although it was a block away, the driver would surely spot him if he glanced in his direction. Rex looked up and saw a shattered window in the building beside him. Without thinking, he jumped onto a crate and then sprang toward the opening. Once safely inside, he watched carefully as the truck crept by. The driver scanned the empty street. It was clear the officer hadn't forgotten their run-in.

Rex backed away from the window. The street wasn't safe at the moment. He'd have to stay put until the man either gave up or continued his search in another neighborhood. Rex scanned the dingy room. The cobwebs on the walls were interrupted only by the sagging wallpaper. At one time, the place must have been an apartment. Now, however, the only furniture in the disgusting room was a grimy couch and a broken-down armchair.

Rex yawned. He wasn't used to so much running around. Sure, he was a big action star, but he only moved when the director yelled, "Action!" When he wasn't performing dazzling stunts, he was resting comfortably in his trailer. He eyed the repulsive couch again and sighed. It wasn't his king-size bed, but it would have to do.

Tentatively, he placed a paw onto one of the vile cushions. It was surprisingly soft. He supposed that was merely his fatigue talking. Whatever it was, he didn't argue. He hopped onto the couch, turned in a circle, then plopped down. A cloud of dust erupted from the cushions. Rex hardly noticed. He was asleep before the dust settled again.

The terrier dreamed he was back in the world he knew. He was back at one of his movie premieres —

Jurassic Bark. He wore a tailor-made tuxedo, his diamond-studded collar, and his meticulously styled hairpiece. He strolled down the red carpet in front of his adoring fans. They shouted his name as he passed. He paused only to give the occasional autograph. Trey stood beside him and held out a small ink pad. Rex placed his paw on the pad, then stamped his paw print in the autograph book of one of the fans.

As Rex proceeded toward the theater, several cameras aimed their lenses at him. The cameras flashed like firecrackers on the Fourth of July. As the flashing lights became brighter and more intense, Rex's dream turned into a nightmare. He was no longer in Hollywood or on the red carpet. He was in a slimy tomato truck. Anything but that. Then his dream shifted once more.

Now he was asleep on a dingy couch in a condemned apartment. However, he wasn't alone. A dark figure crept past him. The man held a small mechanical device. The mechanism had wires running from a tiny watch to a tiny metal box. The man flicked a switch on the device and shoved it under the cushion of the broken armchair. He quickly darted from the room without giving Rex a second glance.

Rex tried to wake from his dream, but he couldn't. He didn't know who the man was or what he was doing there. But he did know one thing — the room began to fill with smoke as the chair started to smolder.

6

Shane sat on the gurney in the back of the truck as Terence drove them to the fire station. When the Dogpatch firehouse came into view, the pain in the boy's chest sank to his stomach. The slim, two-story building looked as if it had sat between two taller buildings at one time. Now, with only vacant lots on either side, the stone building looked more like a small castle than a city facility. Its two small windows above the two large bay doors could have been eyes gazing down at him, adding to its ominous appearance. However, the sight of the firehouse itself wasn't the cause of his pain. Shane didn't look forward to seeing his dad.

When the truck came to a stop, Lionel walked

around to let the boy out of the back. Shane wondered if he was being courteous or just making sure that the boy didn't bolt when he saw daylight. Either way, Shane felt like a prisoner being led out of the back of a police van.

Joe and Pep had old Engine 55 pulled out and were soaping it down. The big red fire truck wasn't one of the latest models. Its rounded nose and older fixtures set it apart from the new trucks roaming the streets today. It had been updated, however, and now carried a more modern extendable ladder on its roof. Either way, it was a perfect match for the old stone firehouse.

As Shane walked up the drive, Joe set down his sponge. The older African American shook his head. "Cap's waiting for you in the locker room."

"And he is seriously angry," Pep added. She didn't even look his way as she aimed the small garden hose at the truck.

"So what else is new?" asked Shane, trying to sound brave.

"Guess you'll find out," Joe said with a smirk. "When you find out about your punishment."

31

This is bad, Shane thought. *If Dad told them what he's going to do to me, it can't be good.*

Shane felt all eyes on him as he shuffled toward the open bay doors. Then Terence was beside him. The rookie put a hand on the boy's shoulder. "Dude, just do what I do. The second he opens his mouth, start crying."

"Tell him it's in your DNA," added Lionel. "That means everything horrible you do is his fault."

Shane glanced at Pep as he passed. "Don't look at me unless you want to hear the truth," she said.

He looked up at Joe before entering the station. "Help me out, Joe," he said. "How do I play this?"

"Play?" Joe frowned. "Just get in there, look him in the eye, and say you're sorry."

Shane trudged inside and headed for the locker room. His dad let him keep a locker like the rest of the crew. When Shane rounded the corner, his locker door was open and his dad sat on the bench in front of it. Connor played with Shane's handheld video game.

"I don't know what to do, Shane," said his dad without looking up.

"That's, um . . . my game, Dad," said Shane.

His father continued to play. "How many times did I warn you about ditching? Three? Four?"

"I . . . I don't remember." Shane stepped forward and held out a hand. "Can you give it to me, please?"

His dad turned off the game and slipped it into his coat pocket. "It's *my* game now."

"Don't do this to me, Dad," Shane pleaded. "Give me one more warning. I won't ditch again!"

Connor closed the locker. "I'm hitting you where it hurts, son. No video games, no TV, and no music. Nothing else seems to work with you."

Shane was about to resort to begging or even crying as Terence suggested. Then the dispatch alarm went off. The air was filled with metallic ringing — there was a fire somewhere.

Connor threw the boy a stern look. Shane raised his hands. "I promise I won't go anywhere. I won't even move."

His dad ushered him out of the locker room. "Oh, you're moving all right."

Shane slid down the pole after his dad. The lower half of the station was alive with movement. The team fumbled over the row of turnout coats, boots, and trousers lining the bay wall.

"Terence, you took my helmet again," Pep scolded as she pulled on her coat.

Terence pointed to his head as he ran by. "This is *my* helmet."

"Then why is my name on it?" asked Pep.

Pep and Terence exchanged helmets while Joe and Lionel fought over some gear as well. Shane stood out of the way and watched the less-than-well-oiled machine that was the Dogpatch Station.

Connor slid his feet into his boots and trousers. "Come on, guys." He glanced at his watch as he pulled the suspenders over his shoulders. "Suit-up should take one minute. No more."

When Connor was dressed, he ushered Shane to the truck. Shane climbed into the back and hugged the wall as the rest of the crew piled in next to him. Joe got behind the wheel while Connor rode shotgun. The large truck roared to life, lunged forward, and then promptly died.

"What's happening?" asked Terence.

"Dumb alternator's shot," replied Joe.

Pep leaned forward. "No, it's the battery again."

"I thought downtown sent us a new one," said Lionel.

"It wasn't new." Connor sighed. "It was *reconditioned*."

Joe tried the key again. Nothing. "Well, you should have sent it back."

"Get out the battery charger," Connor ordered as he climbed out of the truck. "Move, people!"

After three long minutes (a lifetime in firefighters' time), the truck finally started. Its siren wailed as it raced toward the scene of the fire. Luckily, that was only a few blocks away. That didn't stop Dogpatch Station from being the last unit to arrive.

A five-story apartment building was in flames. Fire danced from every window, and smoke billowed from the roof. The black cloud blocked the afternoon sun, giving the surrounding street and sidewalk an eerie cast. Luckily, the building appeared to be abandoned. A large banner stretched across its front — LUXURY LOFTS COMING SOON. As they pulled closer, the banner caught fire and shriveled from the heat. Two fire crews were already on the scene.

Streams of water crisscrossed the building, blasting the hungry flames.

Joe parked across from the large fire truck from Green Point. Beside the truck, Green Point's captain, Jessie Presley, barked orders over her walkie-talkie. Her unit must have been the first to arrive, so she was in charge.

As the Dogpatch team piled out of the truck, Shane looked at the raging inferno through the windshield. He flashed to the nightmare he'd had in school. "Dad . . ."

"Just stay in the rig, Shane," ordered his father. He shut the door behind him.

Shane crawled to the front passenger seat and rolled down the window. He watched as his father ran up to Captain Presley.

"Finished secondary search, Captain," a voice buzzed from her radio. "All clear inside."

The auburn-haired woman sighed and keyed her radio. "Lose your masks and position all crews for exterior attack." She cast a glance toward Connor's team. "That's last place four times in a row,

Dogpatch Looks like you're buying ice cream again."

"Where do you want us, Jessie?" he asked.

"Stand by and we'll see where we need you," she replied, then smiled. "And don't trip over my hoses."

Connor snapped to attention and gave a curt salute. "Yes . . . sir!"

Captain Presley smirked and held up her radio. "Okay, guys, surround and drown."

Relieved, Shane sat back in the seat. His dad didn't have to run into the burning building. He knew that was his father's job, but it scared him nonetheless, especially after what had happened to Uncle Marc.

Shane turned away from the fire and the bad memory. He spotted the Green Point mascot, Sparky, poking her head out of the truck window. The sleek Dalmatian focused on the activity around the building. Another pain hit as Shane realized that he currently sat in place of Dogpatch's former mascot, Blue. It seemed he couldn't escape the memory of what happened that night.

Sparky's whining brought Shane back. The dog stared at the top of the building and barked. Shane squinted through the smoke and saw movement on the roof.

"Dad!" he yelled, pointing to the top of the inferno. "Up there!"

As his father gazed upward, the smoke cleared for a brief moment. A brown dog stood with his front paws on the edge of the roof. His mouth moved, but the roar of the flames overpowered his barks.

Connor turned to his team. "Life net!" he ordered.

The crew scrambled to the truck. Joe, Pep, and Terence pulled out a large red bag while Lionel ran to the ladder control station in back.

Connor climbed onto the truck's roof and onto the ladder. "Lionel, double-time to the roof!" Lionel began to maneuver the captain toward the burning building.

Shane held his breath.

Rex barked at the firefighters below. He relaxed and wagged his tail when he saw them pointing toward him. Then he glanced behind him. He couldn't afford to relax too much; the fire was closing in.

The fire had chased him from the beginning. He had been jarred from his deep sleep on the dirty couch. He had barely escaped before the entire room was in flames. The blaze had quickly spread while he slept. Every exit had been cut off. That left only one place to run — the roof. The fire had consumed the stairwell behind him as he sprinted to the top. Luckily, the roof door was ajar and he ran to the edge. Now the flames roared behind him. Sections of the tar roof bubbled before giving way. Fresh flames rose through the holes they left.

Below him, one of the firefighters ascended on a long white ladder. "Hang on, boy!" yelled the fireman.

As the ladder grew closer, he saw several other firefighters pull something large out of a red pack. Then they backed away from one another, revealing a round life net. It looked like a trampoline with a red dot in the center. They almost had it unfurled when the roof began to crumble under Rex's paws. He couldn't wait any longer.

The dog dove off the roof. But instead of aiming at the net, he soared toward the man on the ladder. He slammed into him, knocking him off balance. The two tumbled toward the ground.

The firefighter safety line caught and his fall was halted. Rex reached out as far as he could and clamped his jaws onto the man's sleeve. His teeth sank into the thick coat as he dangled under the already dangling man.

Rex didn't know how long he could hold on. The firefighter couldn't climb onto the ladder with a heavy dog hanging from one arm. Rex kept his eyes on the man. Reflected in the man's goggles, the dog saw the firefighters position the life net below. That was all he needed to know.

The man's eyes widened as the dog opened his mouth and dropped from his arm. The seasoned stunt dog let his body go limp as he landed on the life net. He felt the surrounding firefighters give it slack to help break his fall. Then they slowly lowered him to the ground.

Rex looked up to see the man pull himself onto the ladder. The ladder then slowly retracted back toward the truck. As it came to a stop, a young boy jumped out of the truck and ran to the man.

"Are you all right?" asked the boy.

"I'm okay," the man replied. He pointed to Rex. "How's the dog?"

Rex felt large hands grab him and lift him off the collapsed net. "Smells like rotten tomatoes," said the owner of those hands. "But he'll live."

As the man and boy walked closer, Rex recognized the young boy at once. It was the kid from the skateboard.

"Oh, no," said the boy. "Not you."

"You know this dog?" asked the man beside him.

The boy nodded. "The mutt from hell."

Rex huffed at the insult. After all, the boy was the one who ran into him. He was about to give the brat a stern bark when a dark-haired woman knelt beside him. She pulled down her goggles and reached for Rex's collar. She examined the small brass tag.

"His name is Dewey," she said. "He's got a name but no address, no phone number."

"I'll call animal control," said another woman. She had auburn hair and held a walkie-talkie.

"We'll handle it," said the man from the ladder.

She playfully elbowed him. "So much for standing by, huh, Connor?" She brought the radio to her mouth and walked away from the crowd. "We've got hot spots on the south side. Let's hustle, guys!"

The man she called Connor pointed to the boy. "Shane, wrap up the dog and put him on the truck."

"Me?" asked Shane.

"Get him on the truck," said Connor. Then he and the rest of his team left to help the other firefighters.

Rex watched as the boy reluctantly grabbed a

blanket from a side compartment. He climbed into the cab and held open the blanket. The dog glanced around and shivered. He supposed he could let the boy wrap the blanket around him (even though it wasn't silk). The terrier hopped into the truck. The boy unceremoniously piled the blanket over him. Rex sat on one side of the backseat while Shane sat on the other.

8

Connor Fahey had insisted on driving the rig back to the station. Driving always helped clear his head. The rest of his team had been quiet during the ride. It seemed as if he wasn't the only one thinking about pulling up last at the scene for the fourth time in a row.

He glanced at the rearview mirror. With the rest of the team piled in, Shane and the dog now sat scrunched up together. Neither one looked happy about it. Connor didn't know what he was going to do about Shane. Connor seemed to be fouling up his job as father just as well as his captain's job.

As they pulled into the station, Zachary Hayden stood in the main bay. Zack was an old friend and had once been a firefighter at Dogpatch. Now he was the city manager. He had traded in his fire suit for a sharp business suit. He tapped some buttons on his PDA as the truck rolled to a stop. Zack closed the cover and shoved the device into his pocket as Connor climbed out of the cab.

"Zack, welcome back," Connor said as the two shook hands.

"Good to see you," said Zack. He patted the captain on the shoulder.

"Why, I haven't seen you since . . ." said Connor.

"Since the memorial," finished Shane as he piled out of the truck.

Zack grimaced. "Yeah. Too long. I've been meaning to come around. . . ."

"Staying for dinner?" asked Pep.

"Who's cooking this week?" he asked.

"Me," Joe announced. "And I made plenty."

Zack looked down. "Um, I better not. I'm a little pressed for time." He leaned close to Connor. "Can we talk?"

"Sure," replied Connor. As Zack started up the stairs, the captain turned to his team. "Pep, get back into that engine. We are not bringing up the rear on another call." He pointed to the others. "You guys clean up the gear and get the truck ready."

Connor noticed Shane edging toward the open bay door. "Shane, you're still on dog duty."

Terence snickered. "He said *dog doodie*." Lionel jabbed him with an elbow. "What?" the rookie asked. "He said it."

Connor followed Zack upstairs and into the bull-pen. As Zack eyed the city map on the wall, Connor grabbed two cups and filled them with what was left of the morning's coffee.

Zack gazed through the large window overlooking the bay. "How's Shane doing?"

"I wish I knew," Connor replied. He handed a cup to his friend. "He doesn't talk to me anymore, unless it's some lame excuse or half-baked lie." Connor sat in his chair and took a sip. "Since Marc died . . . I guess he's just having trouble moving on."

"And what about you?" asked Zack. He nodded toward the city map. "Are these the suspect fires you were talking about?"

"Yeah. And thanks for sending those incident

reports," said Connor. "I know it wasn't exactly protocol."

"No, it wasn't," he replied. "They add up to anything?"

Connor stood and scanned the map. "Not yet. But I think maybe we've got a firebug out there." He took another sip. "And not some random psycho."

Zack sat down. "Connor, the department has experts who handle this kind of thing." He pointed to the closed office across the room. "And last I looked, the captain's office is over there."

Connor glanced toward the dark office, something he didn't do often. A placard on the door read CAPTAIN MARC FAHEY. Connor still hadn't had the heart to move into his brother's old office.

He turned back to Zack and forced a smile. "I like it out here. It keeps me closer to the guys." From Zack's expression, Connor knew he wasn't buying it. The captain changed the subject. "So, if Joe's cooking didn't bring you out here, what's up?"

Zack sighed and set down his cup. "After the mill fire, everybody from the mayor on down was counting on you to fill Marc's shoes." He glanced back to the dark office. "We all expected a period of adjustment. But the last couple of months . . . well, fifty-five was last on scene again today." He stood and paced around the desk. "Connor, if you would have arrived even second to last, it would have gone a long way downtown."

"Hey, you know what would go a long way?" asked Connor. "If downtown didn't send us used batteries and patched-up alternators." Connor stood and opened a file drawer. He pulled out a stack of requisition forms. "Every supply request I make comes back with a big red X through it."

"Your brother would have gone tearing down to the Budget Office and knocked some heads until he got what he needed," Zack replied. "That's the way it works."

Connor slumped back into his chair. A big part of him knew his friend was right. Unfortunately, an even bigger part was in denial. "I'm telling you, somebody downtown has got us in their crosshairs," he said.

Zack sat on the desk. "Budget cuts are hitting

everybody hard. Look, I know you guys have had it rough . . . which makes what I'm about to say that much harder."

Connor didn't look up. "You're replacing me."

"I wish it were that simple," said Zack. "The City Council's advising the mayor to close Dogpatch permanently. If it happens, your territory will be absorbed by Shoreline Station and Green Point."

Somehow, Connor wasn't surprised.

Shane sat on the truck's running board while Pep popped the hood. She climbed onto the front bumper and inspected the engine. Shane cut a disgusted look to the dog beside him. The mutt's coat was matted, dirty, and even singed in some spots. Shane slid away from him. He still reeked of rotten tomatoes.

"Shane," came Pep's voice from under the hood. "Grab my tools, okay?"

"Yeah, sure." He got to his feet and looked back at the dingy dog. "Come on, mutt."

The terrier gave a small snarl and didn't move.

"Suit yourself," said Shane. He crossed to the control panel. He gave a quick turn to the pressure valve. *PSSSSSSSST!* A burst of air shot from the valve. Shane snickered as the dog jumped. The terrier curled his lip at Shane as he trotted into the station.

Shane followed the dog inside, but he didn't care where the mutt went. The boy walked to the back of the bay. The back wall's shelves were full of spare parts, broken gear, and a bunch of rusty equipment Shane didn't recognize. He grabbed a red tool bag from the lower shelf. The heavy canvas bag almost pulled him to the floor before he countered its weight.

As he lugged the bag back to the entrance, he stopped in front of Dogpatch's Wall of Honor. Several faded photos and tarnished placards lined the area. Every firefighter who didn't make it back from a fire was represented. Many of the photographs were in black and white. They showed proud firefighters from the station's early years. The rest were in color, although they had faded over time. The last photo was the newest and therefore the brightest in the lineup. A smiling firefighter with short brown hair rested one hand on a regal German shepherd. The placard beneath it read CAPTAIN

Marc Fahey and mascot Blue. This photo always stood out to Shane; it was his uncle Marc.

"Yo, Shane," echoed Pep's voice. "Today, little bro!"

"Yeah, okay . . ." said Shane. He grabbed the heavy bag with both hands and hustled back to the fire truck.

When he got there, he strained as he held up the bag to Pep. The young woman reached down with one hand and yanked it up with surprising ease. She set it on the fender and rummaged through it.

"So how's it going with that Great Depression report?" she asked.

Shane rolled his eyes. "Good." He rubbed a sore shoulder.

"Oh, yeah?" asked Pep.

"Yeah," he replied. "They've got really good pills for that kind of thing now." He walked back toward the main bay.

"What?" asked Pep.

"Hey, I have to . . . you know . . . go to the bathroom." Shane stepped over several fire hoses as he went back inside.

He carefully made his way to the locker room. Making sure no one saw him, he slipped inside. He quietly moved to his dad's locker. He grabbed the lock and began to spin the dial. Luckily, his dad didn't know Shane knew the combination. With a quiet click, the boy opened the lock and cautiously swung open the door.

Just then, he sensed someone behind him. He cringed and slowly turned. It was the dog they rescued from the building.

Shane breathed again. "Don't you even purr, mutt," he warned. He reached into his father's jacket pocket and pulled out his handheld video game. Just as carefully, he shut the locker door and reattached the lock.

The dog simply stared at him.

Rex could sense that the boy was up to no good. Fortunately, it wasn't any of his business. From the looks of them, none of these people traveled in any of his particular social circles. Therefore, he couldn't depend on them to contact Trey. If Rex were still wearing his hairpiece, maybe they would at least recognize him (he was a household name, after all). But without it, he looked like (he shuddered) any other Irish terrier.

To Rex, there was something even more urgent than contacting Trey, Liz, or his agent — he was starving. He'd fallen from an airplane, almost been burned alive, and dove off a five-story building. Stunts like that work up quite an appetite.

The dog left the locker room in search of food. A place like this had to have some sort of kitchen or dining area.

"Grub's on!" yelled the firefighter named Joe. "Meat stew! Get it while it's hot!"

Rex walked across the open bay, following the man's voice. Rex hoped this *meat stew* contained something remotely edible.

He easily found his way to the mess hall. He simply followed the disgusting smell. He hoped the source of the smell wasn't what these people ate for lunch. When he got to the hall, he saw a steaming pot sitting atop a long dining table. He jumped onto the table and jammed his nose into the pot. Unfortunately, the putrid smell came from within.

"Hey!" yelled Joe. The man came out of the kitchen, holding a wrapped loaf of sliced bread. "What're you doing?"

Rex certainly wasn't eating the slop in the pot. That was for sure. He ducked as the man swung the loaf at his head. The dog scrambled to jump off the table. Glasses and dishes flew in every direction as his paws slipped on the smooth surface. He finally leapt from the table and bolted for the door. As he took off across the bay, Joe was right behind him.

Rex dashed up the stairs toward the bullpen, where Connor and Zack Hayden were in a heated discussion.

"Come on, Zack," said Connor. "You were a fire-fighter once. You were in the trenches. You can't let them shut us down."

"It's not my decision," said Hayden.

"Look, if I'm to blame, don't blame my team," pleaded Connor. "They're the most dedicated, competent, professional . . ."

Rex burst into the room, zipping between Hayden's legs. The man stumbled as the dog left him, tearing into a room with a bunch of large cots lining the wall.

"Whoa!" yelled Zack. "Does that thing have rabies or something?"

Trapped in the crew quarters, Rex turned to face Joe. Rabies? He could do rabies. The dog performed one of his best growls. Joe slid to a stop, dropped the bread, and ran back through the bullpen. Staying in character, Rex gave chase.

"Easy, Zack," said Connor. "He hasn't bitten anybody. . . ."

"Look out!" yelled Joe. "Coming through!" He nearly knocked down the city manager as he ran by.

". . . yet," Connor finished.

Zack leapt onto the desk as Rex galloped through. The dog gave another growl and a loud bark as he chased Joe down the stairs.

The rest of the firefighters had gathered in the bay. Joe ran to them and hid behind Pep. Shane burst out of the locker room, video game in hand.

Rex slid to a stop in front of his audience. He wagged his tail and awaited the applause. It was a brilliant performance, after all. Connor and Zack came down the stairs behind him.

Connor pointed to Shane. "I thought I told you to watch him."

Shane hid the handheld behind his back. "I . . . I did, but he went all psycho."

The firefighters casually slipped out of the bay as Connor marched toward Shane. He passed him and stopped at a cabinet. After some digging, he pulled out an old leather leash. He snapped one end onto Rex's collar and handed the other end to Shane.

"Take him home and make up some 'Found Dog' flyers," ordered Connor. "I want them posted in the morning."

Shane didn't answer. He tugged on the leash, and Rex followed him toward the locker room.

Connor turned to Zack Hayden. "Look, can't you buy us some time to get our performance ratings back up?" he whispered. "One more chance, Zack. You owe us that."

"I'll see what I can do," said Hayden.

Rex trotted beside Shane as the boy slowly skated home. The dog was tired and hungry so he was thrilled as they turned into a driveway in front of a small brick house. He followed the boy to the front door. Shane dug out a key and they went inside.

The home wasn't the lap of luxury to which Rex had become accustomed, but it would do for a while. A tall counter separated the small kitchen from the living room. Past the kitchen, a short hallway led to what had to be the bedrooms.

The boy unclipped the leash, then went to the kitchen. After he made a sandwich for himself, he put everything back into the refrigerator. But before putting away the lunch meat, he looked down at the dog. He sighed and pulled out the remaining slices. "Here," he said, then unceremoniously dropped them onto the floor.

Rex was insulted. Rex was outraged. Rex was offended. But at that moment, he really didn't care. Above all else, Rex was starving. He wolfed down the meat in three gulps.

Shane grabbed his dinner and walked down a short hallway. Moving his sandwich and soda to one hand, he opened a door and disappeared through the doorway. Rex followed him and stopped in front of the room. He couldn't believe his eyes. The boy's bedroom was a mess. Of course, Rex only assumed it was his bedroom because he thought he saw a part of a bed under a mountain of dirty clothes.

Ears back, tail down, Rex tentatively walked into the room. He gazed about in disbelief. Every wall was haphazardly covered in posters (mostly of skateboarders). Comic books and video game cartridges were piled onto every flat surface, with dirty plates and cups piled on top of them.

"Nice, huh?" asked Shane. "Better enjoy it while it lasts."

The dog couldn't help but whimper as he slowly backed out. He didn't sleep in places like that. He'd go back to his couch in the abandoned apartment building if it wasn't burned to the ground.

"What's the matter with you?" asked Shane.

Rex felt his back paw squish into something cold and slimy. He turned around to see his foot resting in a bowl of moldy oatmeal.

Rex snapped. He dashed from the room and sprinted down the hallway. At the end, he dove into another bedroom, a much cleaner one. Yet he couldn't get the sight of the other room out of his mind. He dove under the bed. Then he couldn't stop sneezing. He crawled out from under the bed and looked back at his body. He was covered in dust bunnies. His allergies! Rex rolled on his back. He had to get them off!

Shane ran into the room. "What's your problem?"

Rex stood, shut his eyes, and shook his body as hard as he could. He opened his eyes and froze. He saw the worst thing yet. A floor-length mirror stood at the other side of the room. In the mirror, Rex saw the dirtiest dog he had ever seen. He was horrified even more when he realized it was himself.

Rex ran past Shane and darted out of the bedroom. He ran through the last door in the hallway — the bathroom. He grabbed the shower curtain in his teeth and pulled it back to reveal a small bathtub. Then he went to the sink and pawed open the cabinet. He reached in and pulled out bottles of cleaners . . . medicine . . . there! He found what he was looking for. Rex reached in and grabbed a plastic bottle in his mouth — organic shampoo.

Shane stood in the doorway. "You are one strange dog."

Rex didn't care what the boy thought. He needed to be bathed *now*! He dropped the bottle at Shane's feet and moved to the tub. He reached up a paw and turned the knob. Water began to flow. He turned back, wagged his tail, and barked.

Shane did what the dog wanted. He bathed him thoroughly. Unfortunately, it took four rinses to get out all the bits of tomato from the dog's fur. Then he finished off by blow-drying his hair. Oddly enough, the dog seemed to thoroughly enjoy every bit of it.

When they were done, he led the dog into the living room. He got out his dad's digital camera to take a picture of him for the flyers. However, as Shane raised the camera to his eye, the dog struck a majestic pose. Shane tried again, and the dog struck a cutesy pose. The mutt acted as if he were a super-model posing for a photo shoot. Shane grabbed the dog's collar to hold him still for the final photo. The shot had his arm in the frame but it would have to do.

Shane changed into shorts and a T-shirt and then uploaded the photo to his computer. As he printed out the finished flyers, he heard activity behind him. He turned and saw the weirdest thing. The dog picked up one of his socks from the floor and carried it over to his hamper.

"What're you doing?" asked Shane.

The dog ignored him and continued to pick up the boy's dirty clothes. He meticulously grabbed more socks, shirts, and shorts. He took every item and flung them into the hamper.

"Everything had a place!" Shane got up and tried to pull a pair of shorts from the dog's mouth. "This is my house!"

The mutt planted his paws and shook his head from side to side. Their brief game of tug-of-war ended when the shorts ripped in two. Both the boy and the dog tumbled backward. Shane sat up, holding his half of the torn shorts. The dog trotted over to the hamper and opened his mouth. His half dropped in.

Before Shane could get to his feet, the mutt jumped onto his bed.

"That's it!" said Shane. He jerked on the bed's comforter. It, and the dog on top, tumbled to the floor. Shane stepped over the dog and climbed into bed. "Good night, mutt!" He triumphantly covered himself with the blanket.

As Shane reached up to switch off his lamp, he felt the comforter slide off his body. He rolled over and caught the last of it as the dog yanked it from the bed. Shane got into another tugging match with the cantankerous canine.

"You probably aren't even lost," Shane snarled. "I bet your owner kicked your crusty butt to the curb."

The boy reached to grab more material just as the dog yanked harder. Off balance, Shane tumbled to the floor. With the blanket still in his mouth, the dog jumped onto Shane's back, then onto the bed. He rolled over, wrapping himself like a dog mummy.

"Fine, then." Shane grabbed the pillow from the bed and shuffled to the living room couch. "Sleep well, fur ball. Tomorrow, you are *so* gone."

11

The next morning, Rex followed Shane around town as he did what his father had told him. The dog trotted along on the leash as the boy skated around, stapling flyers onto fences and telephone poles. Rex did not approve of the picture the boy had chosen for the flyer (it clearly wasn't his good side), but he was even more disgusted by the bold text at the top. Each flyer read FOUND: UGLY STINKING MUTT along with the fire station's phone number. Not only were the flyers insulting but, from his years of experience in the business, the slogan was hardly good advertising. Still, the flyers should prove helpful when Trey and Liz extended their search to this part of the city.

Before long, Shane and Rex made their way back to the station. Shane dropped the leash and proceeded up the stairs. Not interested in anything else in the place (especially the kitchen), Rex followed him.

"I need more staples," explained Shane as he walked past his dad in the bullpen.

"Go easy," Connor instructed. "We're running short on everything." The fire captain reached down to pet Rex on the head. Instinctively, the dog pulled away. As a star, he had a strict *no touch* policy.

"Not very friendly for a dog, is he?" asked Connor.

Shane shook his head. "You don't know the half of it."

As the boy dug through a supply cabinet, Rex heard a familiar voice. He padded to the dormitory and saw that someone had left on the television. A woman with blond hair and too much makeup filled the screen. Rex recognized her at once. How could he forget Felicity Hammer? She was the worst entertainment reporter he'd ever had the displeasure to meet.

Rex was about to leave when he froze in his tracks. He stared at the scene behind the reporter. It was *his* house.

"This Beverly Hills mansion was once party central for the A-list crowd," reported Felicity. "But now it is a house of mourning. After an unprecedented manhunt, the search for missing superstar Rex has been called off."

Rex barked and stepped closer.

The screen switched to a series of still images of himself, posing handsomely with his swooping hairpiece. Felicity continued her report. "The number one box office star of such films as *Jurassic Bark* had just launched his own pet-perfume line."

The last still of Rex dissolved into a clip from his commercial. In black and white, Rex trotted past several thin supermodels lounging on stark white steps.

"The fragrance, redolent of bacon, urine, and squirrels," said Felicity, "was considered revolutionary."

Rex placed his paws on the top of the television and barked. He wasn't dead! He was trapped in the middle of nowhere in a dingy fire station, tethered to a spoiled brat. They couldn't just give up the search!

"But sadly . . ." Felicity continued, "the only scent emanating from this once-happy home is the smell of death." Once again, the screen showed her standing in front of his mansion. "Rex's lifetime companion, Trey Falcon, had this to say. . . ."

Trey appeared on the screen. "We'll all remember Rex as the world's most raddest stunt artist ever. Fearless. Amazingly gifted. Always in demand." Trey dabbed at his eye with a tissue. "But that was the problem, wasn't it? He was *always* working. And I'd always say, *Next year, Rex.* Next year we'll nap by a roaring fire. Next year we'll play fetch under a blue moon. Next year we'll do everything a dog and his buddy are meant to do."

Rex howled as a single tear rolled down Trey's cheek. "But there is no next year," continued Trey. "And tonight, there's a bright new star in heaven."

The camera panned back to Felicity. "Thank you, Trey. Memorial services will be . . ." The screen went black.

Rex spun to see Connor set the remote control back onto the coffee table. "Just a waste of electricity," he said. "Thanks for letting me know, boy."

Rex dropped his paws from the television and slumped to the floor. That was it. His Hollywood life had just ended before his eyes.

12

Shane refilled the staple gun and closed the cabinet. As his dad moved to the city map on the wall, the boy glanced at the arson reports splayed across the desk. He looked up to see Connor shove another pushpin into the map. It marked the location of the previous day's apartment fire.

Shane joined him at the map. "Are these all arson fires?"

"Not officially," replied Connor.

The boy pointed to a pin at the top of the small cluster, just north of the station. "But this is the textile mill."

Connor sighed. "Yeah."

"Do you think the fire that killed Uncle Marc was set on purpose?" asked Shane.

"I don't know," replied Connor as he sat at the desk. "You see the same flashover and burn patterns again and again. . . . I just don't know."

"Why would somebody do that?" asked Shane.

"Anger, money . . ." his father replied. "Sometimes just for kicks. You never find out unless you catch the guy."

Shane picked up a photograph from the desk. It showed what was left of a charred wristwatch. "Maybe . . . I can help."

His dad gently pulled the photo from his hand. "Son, it's just a theory. Don't you worry about it." He returned the photo to a folder. "If you want to help, find Dewey's owner, okay?"

Shane smiled. "Okay."

Rex barely noticed Shane enter the room. The boy grabbed his leash and tugged. After the third pull, the dog slowly got to his feet. With no fight left in him, Rex obediently followed the boy down the stairs and out the station. As the boy jumped onto his board, Rex didn't even try to keep up. The leash pulled taut as the dog slowly shuffled along behind him.

"What's wrong now?" asked Shane.

The depressed dog didn't look up.

"If we don't get this done, I can't get rid of you!" said Shane.

Rex didn't know why they even bothered. There was no one looking for him anymore.

The two slowly made their way to the nearby library. As they approached a large kiosk outside, the boy stopped his board and knelt beside the dog. He unclipped the leash and shoved it into his pocket. Leaving the moping dog to keep his own pace, Shane rolled down the sidewalk. He skidded to a stop and pulled some more flyers from his backpack. Rex finally trudged up to him.

"Stay. Sit. Whatever it takes to leave me alone," said Shane. He went back to his pack, pulling out the staple gun.

Rex plopped onto the sidewalk. He let out a deep sigh, not caring about anything in the world.

Then Shane's skateboard slowly rolled down the sidewalk. The dog tracked it with his eyes until it rolled past him. Rex sighed again, and slowly got to his feet. He didn't have anything better to do. His social calendar had been officially cleared forever. The least he could do was help Shane keep up with his board.

As he trotted after the board, it picked up speed. Rex finally had to break into a run to keep up. Overtaking the skateboard, the dog leapt into the air. He came down square on the board. The speed immediately made him feel better. It was a little taste of his former life.

"Hey!" came Shane's voice behind him. Then he heard the boy's footsteps on the hard sidewalk.

Rex didn't care. He put his back paw down and kicked at the concrete. He built up even more speed as he neared the bottom of the hill. For the first time in the past two days, he felt like his old self.

The dog barked as he ollied over the curb. He landed in the street and slalomed past a ditch. The footfalls grew louder behind and Rex turned and wagged his tail at the boy. Shane's eyes widened.

"Look out!" He pointed to something over the dog's shoulder.

HOOOOOOONK!

Rex whipped his head around to see a small car barreling toward him. Without thinking, he pushed off the board and jumped high into the air. The dog somersaulted over the car as it straddled the skateboard on the ground. Just missing the rear bumper, Rex landed back onto the board. He pushed down with his back paws, and the skateboard skidded to a stop. Rex spun it around to see the car continuing down the street.

Eyes wide, Shane stared at him from the sidewalk. "What are you?" he asked. "Some kind of freak-show circus dog?"

Rex barked and wagged his tail. The boy walked over and knelt in front of him. He stared at him for a long time. Then he cocked his head and asked, "What else you got?"

Meanwhile, in another part of town, a map, similar to the one Connor had on the wall at the station, was lying on a grimy workbench. This map was different from Connor's, though, because instead of pushpins there were thick lines of red marker that created an outline of territory near the waterfront — the same area where many of the recent arsons had taken place. A wisp of smoke floated softly toward the termite-infested rafters as a pair of busy hands soldered a vintage Swiss watch mechanism into a fake pack of cigarettes. Although he'd created many of these incendiary devices before, it was dangerous work, and the man had to work carefully. But this time, the firebug was not careful enough.

"Ow!" he cried as he connected a nine-volt battery to the watch's exposed, copper contacts. A bright spark flashed from the device, burning his hand. As the arsonist moved away from his workbench, soothing his sore hand, he turned toward a row of already completed devices — neatly lined up and ready to destroy — and smiled to himself.

13

The next day, Connor strolled across the manicured grass of Mallory Park. Along with the rest of the city's firefighters, he was there to enjoy the annual Firefighters' Picnic. It was a chance for each unit to get to know one another. They would compete in lighthearted firefighting games. The open area was full of all the city's heroes and their families. It was good to take a well-deserved break from their dangerous lives.

He sipped on a cool glass of tea as he made his way back to Dogpatch's table. Then he paused to watch the next contestant in the picnic's main event — the dog challenge course. A golden retriever finished the course by weaving in and out of several small pylons. Then he leapt through a ring of fire.

Zack Hayden stood on a nearby stage. His voice echoed through the PA system. "Give it up for Falstaff from Shoreline Company C."

As everyone clapped, the golden retriever seemed more excited. So excited that he crouched and began doing his business at the finish line. The crowd laughed.

Like any good firefighter, Zack covered for him. "Looks like Falstaff is leaving his *mark* on this course." The crowd laughed. Some applauded. "While our volunteers clean that up, I want to invite up a man whose company, Walking Bud Sports Apparel, has underwritten this entire day. Please welcome Mr. Corbin Sellars."

A thin man in a flashy exercise suit climbed onto the stage. Zack gave him the microphone. "Don't applaud me, I should be applauding you. Listen, I see a burning building, I start running the other way. . . ." The crowd responded with polite laughter. "But seriously, it is the courageous and vigilant spirit of you firefighters protecting this city that amazes me each and every day. I am honored to be sponsoring this event."

As Sellars continued his speech, Connor approached the Dogpatch table. Everyone from his team was enjoying plates of grilled food. Terence joined the table, his plate loaded with four hot dogs. Connor tried not to laugh as he saw the big grass stain on the back of the young firefighter's white Dogpatch shirt. The others snickered, too.

Joe patted Terence on the shoulder. "Went pretty hard in that ladder climb competition," he said. "Good thing you landed on your head."

The team burst into laughter. "Yeah," agreed the rookie. He flicked a few blades from his blond hair.

It made Connor happy to see his team laugh again. He hadn't told them about the impending breakup of Engine 55. He decided he'd wait until after the picnic.

He took another sip of his tea as he ambled toward the trophy table and the most coveted prize of the day — the Golden Hydrant. The large trophy was almost life-size. Engraved at the bottom were all the winners from years past. Most of the winners were Dogpatch Co./Capt. Marc Fahey and mascot Blue.

"You know what, Connor?" said a familiar voice. "I bet your brother's looking down today and smiling."

Connor turned and looked into Jessie Presley's green eyes. He smiled. "Yeah, nothing made Marc happier than kicking Green Point's butt."

Jessie returned his smile, then looked away. She took a deep breath. "Listen, I'm sorry I never called you back after our . . . um . . . our date."

"It's cool," he replied, trying to sound nonchalant. "We both know how it is . . . single parent, the job. You get busy, right?"

"Right, right," she quickly agreed. "Very busy."

"Of course, I think about it quite a lot," he admitted.

"You do?" asked Jessie.

"Sure." He smiled. "And so do you." Connor turned and strolled back to the Dogpatch table. He could feel her eyes on him as he left. He knew she was smiling, too.

"But you didn't come here to listen to some old

quarterback yammer on," Sellars yammered from the stage. "Next up is . . ." Zack leaned in and whispered into his ear. ". . . Sparky of Green Point," continued Sellars. "She's handled by Jasmine JJ Presley, daughter of illustrious Fire Captain Jessie Presley."

Everyone clapped as JJ led the thin Dalmatian to the beginning of the course. Seeing JJ, Connor wondered where Shane had wandered off to. He glanced around but didn't see him.

JJ unclipped Sparky's leash and stood ready at the starting line. When the whistle blew, she signaled the dog to run. And run she did. She practically soared up the small ladder, she ran through a winding flex tube, and she zigzagged between the yellow pylons. JJ ran along beside her, yelling commands.

"Somebody should test that dog for steroids," Pep muttered.

"Really?" asked Terence through a mouthful of hot dog. He swallowed hard. "You think she's juiced?"

Pep rolled her eyes and turned back to the competition.

The Dalmatian dove through the ring of fire and ran past the finish line.

Zack checked his stopwatch. "Sparky takes the lead in a record time of 1:28 . . . eclipsing last year's record set by Blue of Dogpatch Station!"

Lionel put a hand to his face. "Remember the grief we used to give Green Point when Marc and Blue beat their butts year after year?"

"Yeah." Joe stood. "We better blow out of here."

Everyone agreed and stood to leave.

"And now, our final competitor," Sellars announced. "Here is Dogpatch's own Dewey, handled by Shane Fahey, son of Captain Connor Fahey."

The Dogpatch team froze.

"Shane?" asked Connor.

"And the mutt from hell?" asked Joe.

14

The crowd parted as Shane and Rex approached the course. The dog wagged his tail as he scanned the crowd. It was great to be the center of attention again.

The previous day, Rex had performed some of his tricks for Shane. He showed him flips, somersaults, and stunt falls. Rex performed every stunt he could think of that didn't involve a net or a bag. It had been the boy's idea to enter the fire dog competition. That night, the two had snuck to the park and run the course a few times. Rex got it right away. After all, if ordinary dogs could do it, a Hollywood stunt dog could certainly pull it off.

Rex gladly went along with Shane's plan. It was the least he could do to repay him and his father for taking him in (Rex was always kind to the little people). Besides, it felt good to do the thing he loved best — perform!

He and Shane moved to the starting line. The dog crouched and wagged his tail. The whistle was blown and Rex was moving before Shane could finish giving him the signal. The terrier bolted up and over the ladder. He dove into the flex tunnel and rocketed out the other side.

"Dewey's beating Sparky's split time by a full five seconds!" announced Zack.

As he ran, Rex could hear the Dogpatch team cheering him on.

"Go, Dewey!" yelled Connor.

"Bring it home!" shouted Pep.

Like an ace downhill skier, Rex darted through the pylons with ease. The only thing left was the ring of fire. It was a piece of cake for a stunt dog. He focused on the ring and poured on the speed. He was almost on top of it when his focus shifted. He looked through the ring and saw a beautiful Dalmatian standing in front of the crowd. *Lola?* Rex skidded to a halt.

Shane was beside him. "Dewey? What's wrong?"

Rex stared at the dog's spotted coat. He knew the dog before him wasn't his ex-girlfriend. But the memory of Lola struck him like a formula one race car. Rex crumpled to the ground and thought of the last time he'd seen her.

They were on a beach in Monaco. The two love-birds sprawled on beach towels, enjoying the sun and salt air. Lola had stroked his wavy hairpiece and gazed into his eyes. Rex was in heaven.

Later, he had stepped away only for a moment and when he returned, Lola wasn't there. He scanned the area, but she was nowhere on the beach. The longer he searched, the more worried he became. When he finally found her, his worry turned to despair. The slender Dalmatian lay beside a large Afghan hound. His lush flowing hair waved in the breeze as he shared a sausage with the love of Rex's life.

The depressed dog sighed and put his head on his paws.

Zack Hayden blew the whistle. "Game over, folks!" he shouted. "Sparky and JJ Presley win the Dog Challenge!"

The Green Point team cheered and the crowd shuffled to the stage to see them get the trophy. Shane knelt by Rex, but the dog didn't look up. The rest of the Dogpatch team joined them on the field.

"That was so . . . awesome!" Terence shouted.

Pep gave him a high five. "The look on their faces when they thought they were going to lose!"

"Sweetest thing I've seen in months," added Lionel.

Shane clipped the leash to Rex's collar. "Come on, boy, let's get out of here." He led the dog away from the team. Unfortunately, he crossed paths with JJ.

"Go on," said Shane. "Rub it in."

JJ reached down and petted Rex. "I just wanted to say . . . the better dog lost."

15

That night, Shane walked Rex around the neighborhood. The boy had hardly said a word to him after the competition. Since the skateboard incident, he and the boy had gotten along much better. They even seemed to like each other a bit. Now, since Rex failed at the obstacle course, he hoped all that progress hadn't been lost. He had not planned to stay with the Faheys, but now he had nowhere to go.

When they returned to the boy's home, Shane unclipped his leash and strolled into the kitchen. Shane's dad sat on the couch watching TV.

"Hey, where've you been?" asked Connor.

"Just out walking," replied Shane. "Shaking off

the loss." He opened a cabinet and pulled out a bag of dog food. He poured a mound of kibble into a bowl on the kitchen floor.

Connor slapped the couch cushion beside him. "Sit down with your old man. Watch a little football. Like old times."

Shane put away the dog food and joined his dad in the living room. Rex padded up to the bowl and gave it a sniff. He'd been eating the stuff for the past two days. Surprisingly, he started to acquire a taste for the tiny morsels. Now, however, he just wasn't in the mood. He raised his muzzle, sniffing around the kitchen. He heard Connor Fahey laugh in the other room.

"What?" asked Shane.

"Just thinking," he replied. "You know, I haven't seen my team that happy in a long time."

"He could have won, Dad," said Shane.

"He *should* have won," corrected Connor.

Rex moved to the pantry and got a whiff of something wonderful. He aimed his sensitive nostrils over the shelves until he pinpointed the source of the aroma. A bag of beef jerky poked off of the top shelf. He glanced toward the living room. Shane and his dad continued to watch the game.

"Saw you talking to Jessie's little girl," said Connor. "What's the deal with you and her?"

"Come on," said Shane. A hint of embarrassment was in his voice. "She's Green Point, Dad."

"Hey, just asking," said Connor. "Forget I mentioned it."

Back in the kitchen, Rex reached his right front paw to the second shelf. Like a skilled rock climber, he slowly and quietly scaled the pantry shelves. He glanced to the living room. Shane and his dad still had their backs to him.

"Anybody call on those flyers you put up?" asked Connor.

"Nope," Shane replied.

"Give it time."

"I was thinking," Shane said. "I don't know . . . if nobody calls . . . maybe he can stick around awhile."

Rex halted his ascent. The bag of jerky was within reach, but he turned to look in the living room.

"Stick around awhile?" asked Connor.

"Maybe I could take care of him," Shane added.

Connor raised an eyebrow. "You really want to be responsible for this dog?" asked Connor.

Shane thought for a moment, then smiled. "Yeah. Yeah I do."

Rex wagged his tail. Shane wasn't mad at him after all. The dog turned back to the top shelf. And there was no better way to celebrate than with a big bag of tasty jerky. He clamped his teeth onto the bag. He couldn't help but wag his tail harder. Unfortunately, his wagging tail put him off balance. He began to slip. Rex scrambled his paws, trying to keep a foothold. Instead, cans and jars crashed to the floor. The dog tried to hold on, but he only managed to rip open bags of rice and boxes of cereal. With nothing else to do, the dog pushed off from the shelves and landed across from the broken jars of sauce and piles of food. The jerky bag still in his mouth, he looked up to see Shane and his father standing over him.

"You want to be responsible for the dog?" Connor asked Shane. "Okay, you got it."

"But . . ." protested Shane.

"The only *butt* is yours at the station tomorrow." He pointed to the food on the floor. "You're going to work this damage off."

Shane glared down at Rex. The dog gave his tail a tiny wag and did the only thing he could think of. He raised his head, offering to share his jerky. Shane didn't buy it.

16

After school, Shane skateboarded straight to the fire station. As he entered the bay, he saw the dog lying next to the big fire truck. Once again, Pep was buried under the engine's open hood. The dog gave his tail a couple of wags, but Shane didn't stop. He was still mad about the mess he had to clean up the night before.

The boy made his way to the kitchen for a drink (it certainly wasn't for Joe's cooking). Once there, he saw a balding man in a suit and tie. The man had an electronic clipboard similar to the ones he'd seen employees use in grocery stores. The clipboard beeped as the man typed into it. All the while, he scanned the room.

When he looked at the small television set on the counter, Joe waved his hand in front of it. "That TV is my personal property," announced Joe. "And no, I don't have the receipt." The man shook his head and left the room.

"Who's that?" asked Shane.

"Some bean counter sent by the city," Joe replied. He went back to the boiling pot on the stove. "Pretty soon, everything in here will be shipped out to other stations. Including us."

"They shouldn't split you guys up," said Shane, as he grabbed a soda from the refrigerator.

"They can, and they will," said Joe. "Not much of the old neighborhood is left anyway. It's all been boarded up or sold off. I guess there are some things even a fireman can't save."

Shane leaned over the bubbling pot. The smell wasn't as bad as usual. But it looked just as bad. Joe pushed him away. "Hey, your dad said no dinner for you until you mop that engine bay."

"Good to know," Shane muttered as he walked out of the room. He went to the back of the bay and filled the mop bucket. As he wheeled it toward the front doors, the alarm sounded. As usual, it sent a chill down the boy's spine.

Lionel slid down the pole, but before he could move, Terence came down on top of him.

"Ow!" yelled Lionel. "How many times do I have to tell you?! Wait until my feet hit the floor!"

"But you go too slow," Terence snapped. "Let me go first next time!"

Joe ran out of the kitchen, untying his apron. "Hey, lovebirds! Get the lead out!" He threw the apron aside. "What is this, clown school?"

Shane stood out of the way as the team geared up and climbed aboard the engine.

Pep pointed to the front passenger seat. "Guys, check out the dog!"

Shane was surprised to see Rex sitting where his father usually sat. The dog panted happily, ready to go on the rescue.

Connor ran toward the truck and opened the door. "Shane, get the dog off the rig. Now!"

"Down!" ordered Shane.

The dog reluctantly hopped out of the cab. He stood next to Shane as the captain climbed up and closed the door. The engine pulled onto the street, siren blaring.

Shane got the sick feeling every time his dad was called to duty. Without thinking, he reached down and stroked Dewey's head. He never petted him before, but now it eased his mind somehow.

Just then, the dog bolted away from his hand. He barked and tore into the street. He turned right, following the fire truck.

"Oh, crap," said Shane. He grabbed his skateboard and took off after the dog.

There was no way Rex could keep up with the fire truck. Even his keen sense of smell couldn't track the vehicle's scent through winding city streets. Luckily, he didn't have to do either. The echoing siren told the dog exactly which direction it went.

Rex heard Shane skating behind him. The boy had given up calling after him. Now Shane seemed to concentrate on merely keeping up with the sprinting canine.

Rex's chase ended at the entrance of a public utility tunnel. Dust billowed from the large, round opening in the side of a large overpass. Two fire trucks parked in front — Dogpatch and Green Point. Several of the firefighters steadied limping city workers as they slowly emerged from the tunnel.

Rex made it just as Connor approached one of the Green Point firefighters.

"What's the size-up?" asked the captain.

The younger man coughed. "Retrofitters breached the interior pilings. The ceiling's come down fast." He coughed once more. "We got the workers out just in time."

"Where's Jessie want us?" asked Connor.

"My money's on broom detail," the fireman said with a smirk.

Rex sat out of the way and watched the Dogpatch team assist the other firefighters. Shane slid to a stop beside him. Panting, the boy didn't bother to reprimand him. Instead he merely watched as Rex did.

As the rest of the firefighters emerged from the tunnel, Connor glanced around nervously. "Where's Captain Presley?" He grabbed another Green Point team member. "Where's Jessie?" The fireman looked around as well.

Rex cocked his head at the tunnel. Hearing something unusual, he began to move forward. Then something tugged at his collar. It was Shane.

"Oh, no, you don't," said the boy.

Connor and his team edged to the tunnel's entrance. A loud crack echoed through the opening. Mortar and crumbling pieces of concrete fell from the overpass above.

"This whole place is coming down!" said Terence.

"Captain Presley is still in there," said Connor.

"Cap, what do we do?" asked Lionel.

"I'll tell you what we do," said Joe. "We go in there and find her."

Pep slapped the top of her helmet. "Okay, let's do it."

"Pull everybody back," Connor ordered.

"We're not leaving her in there?" said Terence.

"You're staying put," said Connor. Before his team could object, he added, "That's an order!" He pointed to Joe. "Keep the medic close and ready. I'll be on channel one."

As Connor turned on his flashlight, he moved into the dusty tunnel. The rest of his team reluctantly backed away to safety.

Rex pulled harder, but Shane held tightly to his collar. The boy didn't even seem to notice the dog beside him. His eyes were wide with horror as he watched his dad go into the crumbling tunnel. Rex barked. He had to get free. He barked again and Shane glanced down. Rex looked back at the tunnel, then back to the boy. Shane mimicked his actions — looking at the tunnel, then back to the dog. Rex gave another tug, this time keeping his eyes on the boy.

Finally, Rex saw recognition in Shane's eyes. He released the dog's collar. "Be careful," he told him.

Rex sprinted into the dark tunnel. Dust and crumbling bits of mortar rained on his head. He remained focused on the sound he'd heard earlier. He passed several huge mounds of concrete rubble. All of them were easily big enough to bury him or one of the firefighters. However, none of the piles contained the noise he was looking for.

Up ahead, he saw the moving shaft of Connor

Fahey's flashlight. "Jessie!" the man yelled. "Can you hear me?!" Rex darted past him. "Get out of here, dog!" he yelled.

Rex didn't listen. Instead, he made a beeline for the source of the noise. He began to dig at the base of another pile of rubble. He quickly unearthed one of Jessie's gloved hands. The noise he'd heard was the sound of her breathing through her air tank's regulator. She was still alive!

Connor's flashlight beam washed over Rex as he dug. "I said get out of . . ." the man began. Then the beam came to rest on Jessie's hand. Connor dropped to his knees, helping Rex dig. Before long, the two had removed the rocks and debris from atop Jessie's body.

Connor grabbed the unconscious woman in both arms and stumbled toward the mouth of the tunnel. Rex sneezed as dust filled his lungs. He galloped toward the dim light of the tunnel's entrance. Twice he stopped and barked back at Connor so the man could follow the sound.

As they neared the light, another loud crack

echoed through the tunnel. It was followed by a rumble that grew louder and louder. Rex sprinted toward the exit and was happy to hear that Connor had picked up the pace. The three of them burst into the bright sunlight as the tunnel collapsed. A plume of dust shot out from the rubble. The rest of the firefighters cheered. They were safe.

Green Point's team took Jessie from Connor's arms. They strapped her to a gurney and placed an oxygen mask over her face. Rex's tail wagged when he saw her stir into consciousness. With a weak smile, she reached toward Connor and took his hand.

A local news reporter and cameraman arrived. The brown-haired woman first approached the Dogpatch team tending to the dazed utility workers. They exchanged a few words, and then, in unison, the entire team pointed toward Rex. The woman quickly shuffled over to the dog, Connor, and Shane.

"Is that the dog who saved the day?" asked a reporter. She motioned for her cameraman to get a shot of the dog.

Connor smiled. "That's him."

"Who does he belong to?" she asked, thrusting a microphone toward the captain's face.

Connor glanced at Shane and grinned. "Engine Fifty-five. He's the mascot of Dogpatch Station."

She knelt beside Rex. "Smile, wonder dog. You made the news."

As the camera lens moved closer, Rex angled his head, making sure they shot his *good* side.

17

Over the next few days, Connor, Shane, and Rex had been interviewed by the rest of the local stations. Rex's story was picked up and aired by the major news channels as well. The dog was a national celebrity again. Granted, he wasn't known for being Rex, the top-grossing action stunt dog. He was known for being Dewey, Dogpatch firehouse dog and bona fide hero.

During Dogpatch's last two weeks before reassignment, Rex often slept on a special cushion in the firehouse dorm. Whenever an alarm would sound, the dog was the first on his paws. He ran to each bed and pulled away the blankets with his mouth. The firefighters would spring off the cots and slide down the fire pole. Rex had considered sliding down the pole as well. However, each time he ended up chickening out and taking the stairs. It was a stunt he'd never been trained for.

He took his job as firehouse dog very seriously. He rode to every emergency, sitting right up front with Connor. At the scene, he would always help as best he could. He'd locate trapped victims, warn the firefighters of unstable structures, and even carry water to each of them when the job was through. Of course, he had a little help from a special pack that Terence made for him.

At night, Rex slept right in bed with Shane. The two were becoming the best of friends. The dog would help tidy up their room, and Shane would sneak him special snacks from the kitchen. Oftentimes, Rex helped the boy with his schoolwork. If Shane played video games before studying, Rex would reach out his paw and press a button on the controller, messing up his game. Shane's annoyance didn't last too long. He would pat the dog on the head, then go to his desk and study. Shane didn't even ditch class anymore.

Rex was very comfortable in his new life. He enjoyed being a hero, a best friend, and, more than anything, Rex enjoyed being a regular dog for a change.

During their last night, Rex watched as the Dogpatch crew began to pack up the firehouse. Gear was cataloged, personal belongings were gathered, and photos from the Wall of Honor were carefully packed into boxes. The entire team was surprisingly lighthearted. Even if it had only been for a couple of weeks, they had all worked together as a team should.

Lionel pulled down the last newspaper article tacked to the bulletin board. A photo of Rex and the rest of the team sat above the article.

"Figures," Lionel snorted, "we finally get our act together" — he carefully folded the article and placed it in a cardboard box — "just in time to close."

"Late as usual," said Pep. "That's us."

"At least we went out swinging, right?" asked Joe. Everyone agreed. Joe pulled a plastic mounted lobster from the wall. "Hey, Shane, can I have your talking lobster?"

"Sure," said Shane. "If I can have your football stein."

"Deal," agreed Joe.

A maroon sedan pulled up to the open bay doors. Zachary Hayden got out carrying several plastic grocery bags. "Did someone order rocky road?"

Connor Fahey walked down the stairs. "Parting gift, Zack?"

Hayden set the bags on a nearby table. "Courtesy of Green Point. I told them I was coming over here on business anyway."

Rex placed his front paws on the table and sniffed the bags. He loved rocky road.

"I prefer to give bad news in person," continued Hayden.

"You've got our reassignments?" asked Joe.

"Afraid not," he replied.

"What is it?" asked Terence. His brow furrowed. "Pink slips?"

Zack shook his head. "Nope."

Connor crossed his arms. "So what's the bad news?"

"Bad news is that you're going to be up all night" — he shook his head — "unpacking all this stuff."

Rex left the ice cream and dropped to all fours. He was as dumbfounded as the rest of the team looked.

Zack broke into a wide grin. "The order came down from the mayor himself. Dogpatch is staying put." He pointed to Rex. "That furry little publicity magnet saved this company's rear end."

The team cheered. Lionel and Terence exchanged a high five. Pep even gave Hayden a big kiss.

Connor stepped up and shook his friend's hand. "Shane was right. Maybe all Dogpatch needed was a good dog."

The next day after school, Shane raced to the fire station. He had some great news. As he propped his board by the open bay doors, he heard the usual clanking of pots from the kitchen. He wanted to tell his dad first, but he couldn't wait. He had to tell someone. He ran straight for the kitchen while he dug through his backpack.

"Joe, check this out," he said, pulling out a piece of paper. "B-plus on my science quiz."

Joe leaned across to get a closer look while he whisked something in a bowl.

"Kid, I'm impressed." Then his smiled disappeared. He glanced both ways and leaned closer. "Did you copy?"

"No!" Shane laughed. "I studied for almost one whole night."

Then Shane noticed a strange smell in the kitchen. Oddly enough, it kind of smelled like . . . food. "Wait, are you actually cooking real food?" he asked.

Joe frowned and stirred faster. "It's not a moon launch. It's a cannoli." He turned his back as Shane tried to get a closer look at the bowl. "Get out of here," Joe barked.

Shane laughed and ran upstairs to the bullpen. He saw Lionel sitting behind his dad's desk. "Is my dad here?"

"He's at a meeting downtown," said Lionel. He turned the page of his newspaper.

Shane noticed that the desk was bare. "Where's his stuff?" he asked.

Lionel nodded to something across the room. Shane caught his breath when he saw Uncle Marc's office door open. All of his uncle's things were gone. Now his father's belongings sat on the desk, lined the bookshelves, and hung on the wall.

"What's wrong with his old office?" asked Shane. He gestured to the old desk in the bullpen.

"He's captain," replied Lionel. "That's where he belongs." The man put down his paper and sat up. "Look, I know I said blame your DNA for all your problems. So go ahead, be mad at him if you want, but he's finally stepping up." Lionel gestured to the science quiz in the boy's hand. "And it looks like you have, too."

Shane didn't answer. He knew that Lionel was right. He wasn't mad at his father for moving into his uncle's office. It was the captain's office and his dad was the captain. And from what he'd seen in the past two weeks, he was going to be one of the greats.

Shane slowly walked toward the open office. As he peeked inside, he got another surprise. Dewey was sprawled out on a brand-new dog bed. A brass nameplate was bolted to the wall behind him. DEWEY, ENGINE 55 MASCOT.

Shane couldn't help but laugh. "Make yourself right at home."

As he stepped inside the room, he saw an unpacked box. It was jammed full of memos, news clippings, and report folders. He pulled out a folder, and a familiar photo fell to the ground. It showed the charred face of a wristwatch. These were his dad's arson files. As he bent to grab the photo, he thought of an idea.

That night, Shane finished inputting the final set of coordinates as his dad got home. Dewey wagged his tail and trotted out to greet him. A moment later, he returned to the boy's room with Connor close behind.

"Guess what?" his dad asked. "The Public Affairs Office called. The mayor wants you and Dewey to appear at the firefighters benefit. Cool, huh?"

"Yeah," agreed Shane. He closed the current report and pulled the next one off the pile nearby.

"What's going on?" asked Connor.

"I'm trying to get you organized," Shane said as he tapped a few keys on the keyboard. A map of the city appeared on the computer monitor. Using his mouse, Shane zoomed in on their neighborhood. Several red fire icons flashed throughout the map, representing the locations of the recent fires.

"Wait a minute, that's my . . ." his dad began. Then he leaned closer to the monitor.

"Basically I uploaded the coordinates from your

wall map onto a satellite imaging database," Shane explained. "Anyway, it beats pushpins." He turned to his father, expecting approval. Instead, his dad grimaced.

"You shouldn't have done all of this," he said.

"Sorry," Shane said. "I just wanted to help."

His dad placed a gentle hand on his shoulder. "No. What I'm saying is . . ." He pointed to the files spread about the room. "This should never have been your responsibility."

Sliding a stack of reports to one side, Connor sat on the boy's bed. Shane swiveled his chair to face him.

"For the past six months, I have been ragging on you," explained his dad. "When the truth is, I'm the one who's neglecting what's important."

"What's that?" asked Shane.

"You," his dad replied.

Dewey jumped onto the bed next to his father. Some files crunched under his paws, but no one seemed to mind. He plopped down and placed his head in the man's lap.

Connor scratched the dog behind the ears.

"Shane, you're so smart and capable and strong. And I've been so lost in all this since Marc died. . . ." He hung his head. "I guess I turned into a pretty lousy dad. And I'm sorry." His eyes met Shane's. "Okay?"

". . . Okay," Shane said quietly.

The two sat silently for a moment. His dad's words echoed in Shane's mind. Thinking of them made his throat clench and his eyes well with tears.

Finally, his dad broke the silence. "Thanks for this."

Shane jumped to his feet and desperately tried not to cry. "But I'm not strong," he croaked. "I'm weak. And I'm a bad person."

"Why would you think something like that?" asked Connor.

Shane faced the opposite wall and wiped his face with his shirtsleeve. "The day of the warehouse fire, I was at school when the trucks drove by. . . ." He stopped and took a few deep breaths. Thankfully, his dad didn't interrupt. "But then JJ called her mom and heard that a firefighter was missing. . . ."

Shane remembered that day vividly. That was the first time he ditched school. Not even pausing to pull his board out of his locker, he had run from school all the way to the station. When he got there, the truck was back and everyone on the team was quiet.

"No one would look at me," he continued. "Not Lionel, not Pep, not Joe . . ." He took another breath and wiped his face again. "That's when I knew you were dead."

Finally, Shane found the courage to turn around. His father stared at him from the bed. Even Dewey gazed at him, showing concern. "I loved Uncle Marc," said Shane. "But when I found out it was him . . . part of me was . . . happy." Tears streamed down his cheeks. "I was happy because it wasn't you."

Connor stood and hugged his son. Shane wrapped his arms around his dad and sobbed into his chest.

"It's all right," reassured his dad. "People go through a wide range of emotions in stressful times." He rubbed a hand across his son's back. "In those times, emotions and thoughts can attack us from every direction. They seem inappropriate and we feel guilty later." He held his son at arm's length and looked him in the eyes. "I assure you, it's completely normal."

"Yeah?" Shane whispered.

"Yeah," his father replied. He pulled his son close again. "We're going to get past this," he reassured. "I promise. You and me . . . together."

Shane felt something against his leg. Dewey leaned against him. The terrier looked up and wagged his tail. The boy smiled and rubbed the dog's head.

"Now come on." His dad released him. "Get some sleep. Big day tomorrow." He pointed to Dewey. "You and your wonder dog here have to put on your show for the mayor."

His dad turned off his computer while Shane and Dewey cleared the files from the bed. After he and the dog had settled in, his dad switched off the light and left them alone. His father's words echoed in his head. *We're going to get past this.* Shane closed his eyes and knew it was true.

19

Applause echoed through the large banquet hall, waking Rex from his nap. He sat up beside Shane's chair at the Dogpatch table. The rest of the hall was filled with firefighters, City Council members, and much of the city's elite. Everyone was formally dressed as they came to honor the city's firefighters.

Of course, this wasn't his first formal event. Throughout his career, he had been to many black-tie award ceremonies. This one wasn't *quite* as boring as those had been. It was almost like old times. The only thing he was missing was his trademark hair-piece. Actually, that wasn't true. Rex didn't miss it at all.

Corbin Sellars waited for the applause to die

down. "I just got the tally. This little reception's raised over one hundred thousand dollars for our firefighters. Not bad, huh? Give yourselves a round of applause." The hall filled with applause once more. "And while you're at it, how about something for our honored guests from Dogpatch Station, Engine Fifty-five!" The applause grew louder. There were even some whistles thrown in for good measure.

At the Dogpatch table, Zack Hayden clapped loudly. He leaned over to Connor. "Now maybe we can squeeze a new battery out of the department."

"Thanks for pleading our case with the mayor," said Connor.

"Don't thank me." He looked down at Rex. "Thank Supermutt."

Joe glanced at the only empty seat at their table. "Where's Pep?" he asked. "We're almost on!"

Lionel craned his neck, looking around the hall. "Here she comes." His eyes widened. "And she is *way* out of uniform."

Pep entered the hall wearing a tight, sparkling red evening gown. Normally pulled back in a ponytail, her long brown hair shimmered and flowed over her bare shoulders. Rex wagged his tail. Pep looked better than many of the Hollywood starlets he'd worked with in the past.

The rest of her team stood as she approached. Terence even pulled out her chair. "Since when are you a girl?" he asked.

Pep slapped his hand off the chair and quickly took her seat. "Stop staring," she snapped. "You'll burn holes."

Everyone quickly turned their attention back to the main stage. "Let's get to the real reason we're here," continued Mr. Sellars. "This little pooch has been on all the major news channels, newspapers, and all five local news channels. Please welcome the pride of Engine Fifty-five: Dewey the Wonder Dog and his boy, Shane Fahey."

Rex leapt to his feet. He was on! As the audience clapped once more, he happily trotted behind Shane. They winded through the round banquet tables and climbed up the stairs and onto the stage. Corbin Sellars handed Shane the microphone, then stepped back and joined in the applause.

The noise died as Shane brought the mike to his lips. "Hey, everyone. Before I get to Dewey's more radical moves, I'd like to start with something simple. First, I need a volunteer." He glanced back at Corbin Sellars. "How about you, Mr. Sellars? Do you have a wallet or watch or something you carry on you?"

Sellars stepped forward and slipped the watch off his wrist. He smirked at the audience. "I'm going to get this back, right?"

"We hope," said Shane. A smattering of laughter rippled through the audience.

Shane held the watch in front of Rex's nose. The dog gave it a couple of good sniffs, memorizing its scent. Then he turned his back to the audience and lay on the stage. He placed his front paws over his eyes.

Behind him, he heard Connor walk to the foot of the stage. Shane would hand the watch to his father as planned. Then Connor would hide it somewhere in the hall.

"Hide it good now, Captain," came Joe's voice from the crowd.

"A firehouse mascot isn't just for show," Shane explained. "It's a real job requiring real skills. Special skills." After a brief pause, Shane turned to the dog. "Okay, Dewey. Find it!"

Rex sprang to his feet and leapt off the stage. He began to sniff along the floor of the banquet hall. He moved under tables, sniffing the freshly polished shoes of several of the guests.

"Dewey's sense of smell is ten thousand times more powerful than a human's," said Shane. "That, combined with the ability to think on his paws, makes him an invaluable search-and-rescue dog."

Rex ran to another table. The scent was growing stronger. He was quickly homing in on the hidden watch. Then he smelled something vaguely familiar. It wasn't the watch but a scent that hadn't entered his nostrils in a long time. Intrigued, Rex kept his nose to the ground and followed the new trail. He quickly found the source of the smell. A pair of designer sneakers were planted between two of the banquet tables. Rex looked up and couldn't believe his eyes. He wagged his tail.

"It really is you!" said Trey Falcon. He dropped

to the floor and gave the dog a big hug. "I missed you, dude! Wow, did I miss you!"

Shane jumped off the stage and followed his dad down the aisle. They came to a stop beside Rex and his old friend.

Trey stood and shook the boy's hand. "You must be Shane Fahey. I saw your picture in the paper."

"What's this about?" asked the captain.

Trey's eyes welled with tears. "I don't know how and I don't care!" He crouched and hugged Rex again. "You found my dog!"

Shane still couldn't believe what he was hearing. This strange man appeared out of nowhere and claimed Dewey was his dog. He introduced himself as Trey Falcon from Hollywood. Connor had quickly ushered them to a quiet corner of the hall. They sat at an empty table, Dewey sitting between Shane and Trey.

Trey reached into his messenger bag and pulled out a small portfolio folder. He opened it and removed a clipped newspaper article. "I was crazy bumming. Then I saw his picture in the paper." He handed it to Shane. The photo depicted Shane kneeling, with his arm around Dewey. "Dudes, I couldn't believe it!"

Trey flipped through several pages in his portfolio. There were posters from movies like *Terrier at 20,000 Feet* and *Dog Day Afternoon 2: Electric Boogaloo*. Each poster listed a dog named Rex as the star. And each poster showed an Irish terrier in an action pose. The dog looked just like Dewey, but the dog on the posters had a swooping Mohawk hairdo.

"This dog is no . . . actor," said Connor.

"You *must* have seen him in *The Fast and the Furriest*," Trey said, flipping the page. The movie's poster showed the same dog running beside a race car. "Come on, that's a Rex classic!"

"His name isn't Rex," Shane protested. "It's Dewey. It's on his tag." He pointed to the dog's plain leather collar.

Trey laughed. "That's just a prop tag he was wearing when he got lost."

"Look, Mr. Falcon." Connor leaned in. "He's no movie star. He's not a celebrity. He's a mutt. We practically found him on the street."

"Well, you see . . . he looks different in these posters because his trademark Mohawk is"

— he lowered his voice to an animated whisper — "a hairpiece."

Shane examined the dog in the portfolio again. The dog did look like Dewey with a hairpiece. But he shook his head. He wouldn't believe it. Dewey was just an ordinary mutt.

"Come on," said Trey. "Surely you must have noticed how special he is."

Shane's throat tightened. Dewey may be a mutt, but he was truly far from ordinary. Mr. Falcon had to be right. Shane looked into his dad's eyes and realized that he had come to the same conclusion.

"Mr. Falcon," said Connor. "I appreciate what you've been through, but this dog means a lot to the fire company, this city . . . and especially to my son." He reached into his jacket. "If there's any way we can compensate you . . ."

Trey gasped. "If you're asking me to put a price on family, I can't." He reached into his bag and pulled out a leash. "It's time for Rex to come home."

Shane leapt to his feet. "You can't take him away!"

"Shane . . ." His dad put a hand on the boy's shoulder.

"Dad, don't let him!" Shane pleaded.

Connor stood beside his son. "It's his dog, Shane. We don't have a choice."

Trey bent over and clipped the leash onto the dog's collar. "This probably won't mean much now, but thanks for taking care of him."

"You've got it wrong," replied the captain. "He's the one who took care of us."

Shane watched as Dewey, no, Rex, hopped to his feet. The terrier nuzzled Shane's leg and licked his hand.

Shane jerked away from him. "Get out of here, then! Just go." Tears streamed from his eyes as he glared at Trey. "Take him! He was just a big pain anyway!"

The few guests that were left stared at the scene, but Shane didn't care. He watched as Trey Falcon led the dog away. Just before exiting the main doors, the dog looked over his shoulder. Their eyes met briefly before Trey tugged the leash. Then they were gone.

Connor pulled him close. "I was going to say something wise and fatherly. But the truth is . . . this just stinks."

21

Shane slumped in his chair at the Dogpatch table. Most everyone was gone except Engine 55's team. They sat quietly as the servers cleaned up around them. A few of them began to say some comforting words to Shane and one another. However, each time they tried, nothing ever sounded right.

The silence was broken when Pep came running into the hall. She hopped the last few steps as she struggled to pull off one of her high-heeled shoes. "Cap, we've got an EMS call!"

As the team sprang to their feet, the captain placed a hand on Shane's shoulder. "Come on, son. I'll find you a ride."

"Just go." He shook off his father's hand. "I've got my board."

"Shane . . ."

Shane didn't look up. "I'll see you at home."

His father stood there a moment longer, then ran to join the others.

The boy stared across the room when his eyes fell onto a floral arrangement in the center of another table. He stood and paced toward it. He reached into the arrangement and pulled out Mr. Sellars's watch. His dad had hidden it there for Rex to find. He turned the watch over in his hands. The antique face seemed familiar somehow. The name at the bottom of the face read BOUTINE.

Then it hit him. The watch was identical to the ones he'd seen in the crime scene photos. He remembered a charred and melted watch face. It was almost unrecognizable. Only the watchmaker's name, BOUTINE, could be read on the face.

Suddenly, the watch was yanked from his hand. "Thanks," said a voice beside him. Shane left his memory and looked up to see Corbin Sellars. The man slid his watch back onto his wrist. "And hey," he said. "I'm real sorry about your dog. Can I buy you another one?"

"Another one?" asked Shane. His mind raced.

Sellars tousled the boy's hair. "You think about it."

Shane watched the man amble out of the ball-room. Could Sellars be connected to the fires somehow? Shane was determined to find out. He followed the man through the main doors and into the large corridor beyond. Then Shane fell back as Sellars stopped, glanced around, and ducked into a service entrance. Once the door shut, Shane ran down the hallway and slowly pushed it open.

Through the small opening, Shane could see several wheeled racks of linens and tableware crowding the small storage area. He could also see the back of Sellars's head.

"What's the holdup?" Sellars asked.

"More activity in that area right now is sure to draw attention," said another voice. "And I'm not just talking about Connor Fahey."

Shane pushed open the door a bit farther. He leaned in as much as he dared, but he still couldn't see the owner of the voice. The mystery man stood behind another rack of linens.

"I finally put a City Council in place that will approve a sports complex," growled Sellars, his genial nature all but vanished. "I want that last property in ashes. Do it tonight."

"Tonight?" asked the other man. "How am I going to do that?"

"You're the fireman," barked Sellars. "Figure it out. Light a match."

Shane closed the door and glanced around. His dad was right. The fires were set deliberately. Worse than that, they were set by a firefighter.

Shane cracked open the door again. He had to find out who the other man was. Unfortunately, the room was empty. He spied another door on the other side and dashed through. He ran down a service corridor and came upon a glass exit door. Outside, Corbin Sellars pulled away in a silver sports car. Another plain sedan left the parking lot behind him. Unfortunately, Shane couldn't see who drove that one. He couldn't see the identity of the fireman firebug.

22

Rex could eat only half a helping of Kobe beef. He'd forgotten how much he loved it. Unfortunately, it no longer loved him. The rich meat seemed to sit in his stomach like a rock. He trotted to his crystal water dish and lapped up some water. The carbonation of the sparkling water tickled his nose and made him sneeze. He'd forgotten about that as well.

He shook his head and hopped onto the hotel room's king-size bed. As he relaxed, his stomach gurgled.

"Dude, what were they feeding you?" asked Trey. "Kibble?"

Rex stretched out across the spacious bed.

He wasn't used to so much room anymore. It was very nice.

After they had left the banquet hall, a limo carried them to a nearby luxury hotel. Even his last producer, Liz Knowles, was there. From what Rex could tell, Liz and Trey had grown quite close during his absence.

Once in the room, Rex was treated to every luxury he had missed since his stay at the Faheys'. His prop collar had been replaced by his diamond-studded collar. Then he'd been given all the Kobe beef he could eat, although he couldn't eat much. But once the dog ate his fill and lay on the bed, he couldn't get the Faheys out of his head. Especially Shane.

Liz rubbed Trey's shoulders. "This is so unreal, Trey."

He put his hand on hers. "I'm telling you, deep down I knew it was going to take more than a mountain to stop Rex. Right, buddy?"

The dog gave his tail a couple of wags.

"So what are you going to do first?" asked Liz.

Trey stood and moved to the center of the room. "First, a press conference. I have the whole campaign figured out." He slowly waved his hands in front of him. "Rex: Back from the Boneyard!"

"What?" asked Liz.

Trey rubbed his chin. "You're right. Too scary for our younger viewers."

"What about all those things you said?" asked Liz. "Playing fetch, hiking, treating him like a real dog, remember?"

Trey waved a dismissing hand. "Hey, as soon as word gets out, his fee will double. But next year, I promise . . ."

"Next year, Trey?" asked Liz.

While the two bickered, Rex hopped down and trotted to the open window. The cool breeze that ruffled his wavy hairpiece also blew in the sounds of the city below. Without thinking, his tail wagged as he wondered what Shane was up to.

"Listen, I know Rex," Trey argued. "He doesn't want to be a *real dog*, he wants to be a star! He's dying to leap back into action. Right, boy?"

Rex's tail stopped wagging. A shrill noise pierced

through the rest of the city's sounds. As it grew louder, Rex recognized it and barked.

"See," said Trey.

The sharp wail of the siren filled Rex's ears. He poked his head out the window and saw a large fire engine speeding through the streets below. As it approached the hotel, Rex saw that it wasn't just any fire engine. It was Engine 55, the Dogpatch team. Rex barked louder.

"Chill, dude, it's just a siren," said Trey.

Rex had to do something. His crew needed him. He glanced down at the street, then pulled his head inside. Next he stepped back and ran for the open window.

"Rex!" shouted Trey.

It was too late, he flew through the window and into the night air. As he fell, he aimed for the large hotel awning below. Turning at the last moment, his back hit the taut cloth. It sprang back and catapulted him to the side. Rex's hairpiece flew away, but he didn't care. He flailed his legs, rotating himself again. He landed atop a pile of suitcases on a hotel luggage cart. Bags splayed everywhere as they broke his fall.

The dog kicked off and landed on the hard pavement. He was already running after the truck when he hit the ground.

Rex barked as the engine gained speed and began to pull away. Then he saw the captain's shocked expression in the side-view mirror. A moment later, the fire truck slammed on its brakes. The dog sprinted for the opening passenger door.

"Get on, boy!" said Connor.

Rex leapt into the cab and took his usual seat beside the captain. Terence hit the gas and they sped into the night.

23

Shane ran up the stairs and burst into his father's office. He snatched up the phone and called his dad's mobile. The call went straight to voice mail. Shane hung up and called JJ Presley.

"Hello?" came JJ's voice on the phone.

"JJ, is your mom there?" Shane asked. "I can't get my dad on the phone."

"She's at the harbor," the girl replied. "There's a monster blaze down there."

"I think it's arson," said Shane. "I think they set it on purpose!"

"Wait, Shane, slow down," she said. "What are you talking about? Who?"

Shane took a deep breath and plopped into his

dad's chair. "I heard Corbin Sellars talking about burning buildings to make way for a stadium. They want to buy up all the land."

"But why would they be burning down a garbage barge?" she asked. "It's not even land."

Shane leaned forward. "Okay, that's true." He moved his dad's computer mouse. The screen blinked on. "Hang on, I've got an idea." He propped the phone on his shoulder, using both hands to type.

Shane had transferred the satellite image and data to his father's computer. There hadn't been another local fire, so there were no new coordinates entered. He pulled up the familiar map of their neighborhood. The same fire icons marked locations of the suspicious fires. They were scattered about the area, about the right size for a sports center.

"What are you doing?" asked JJ.

"Joe told me the whole neighborhood's been boarded up, or sold off. . . ." Shane said as he typed. He identified the remaining buildings in the area. After plugging in a few addresses on the Internet, he learned that all of them had been sold recently.

However, he didn't have to look up who had bought them.

"What is it, Shane?"

Shane kept looking up addresses. "Everything in the neighborhood has been either sold or burned down." He brought back the satellite image. Sitting right in the middle was . . . "Everything but the firehouse."

Shane leapt to his feet. "The barge is a decoy. The last target is . . . it's right here! It's Dogpatch!"

Just then, a small clatter sounded from the darkness below. Shane crouched behind the desk. "JJ, I think someone's downstairs."

"Shane, get out of there now!" she yelled.

He didn't reply. He turned off the phone and quietly set it on the desk. Whoever had been starting fires was about to start one in the fire station. However, there was something more important than stopping this firebug from burning down his dad's workplace. Whoever the arsonist was, he set the fire in the mill, the one that killed his uncle Marc. Shane wasn't going to let him get away with it.

As Shane stepped out of the office, he heard movement on the stairs. He quickly ducked into the dorms and slid under one of the cots. Before long, the footsteps echoed in the bullpen. He held his breath as a man entered the room. Shane angled his head under the cot, but all he could see were a man's legs. His back to Shane, the man strode to the laundry alcove. The firebug crouched, reached into his sport coat, and pulled out an odd device. He set the device on the dryer, then he grunted as he pulled the dryer away from the wall, revealing the vent tube and the gas line. Shane didn't get a clear look at the apparatus, but he definitely recognized the small watch attached to it. The man reached behind the dryer and pulled out the vent tube. A cloud of dust and lint filled the air as the man did something to the device and then shoved it into the tube. He replaced the tube and the dryer.

The man stood and surveyed the dorm. That's when Shane got a good look at his face. The boy gasped. It was Zack Hayden.

Surprised, Shane shuffled farther back under the cot. He watched Hayden step closer and closer. He stopped inches away from the boy's hiding place. Then he turned on his heels and jumped onto the fire pole. He slid down and out of sight.

Shane scrambled out from under the cot. He dashed through the bullpen toward the stairs. There was no way he could take on Hayden by himself. He needed a weapon of some kind. Then Shane saw just what he needed. It was very fitting as well.

The boy ran down the stairs as quietly as he could. He darted across the bay and found Hayden in the kitchen. The man checked his watch, then grabbed one of Joe's cannolis. Just as Hayden brought it to his open mouth, Shane blasted him with the fire extinguisher.

Hayden coughed and scrambled to clear his eyes. Covered in white flame retardant, he shook his head and looked at Shane. His eyes widened. "What are you doing here?" he asked.

Shane moved closer, keeping his hand on the trigger. "You set the fire that killed my uncle!"

Hayden shook his head. "He died in the line of duty." He coughed again. "Come on, Shane, put that down."

Shane sneered. "No! You did it!" He moved closer. "Why did you do it? To build a football stadium?"

"Shane, you're having trouble separating fact from fiction." Hayden checked his watch. "Put that thing down and let's talk outside."

"I'll put it down when the police get here," Shane said. "Which should be any minute."

Hayden pointed to him and smiled. "See? You're lying again."

Shane prepared to give him another blast. That's when the wall exploded.

24

Rex watched as Dogpatch and Green Point attacked the garbage barge. Black smoke rolled off the thirty-foot flames and filled the night sky. Engine 55 had been the first on the scene, so Connor called the shots. He placed his and Green Point's firefighters in strategic positions to drench the flames with thick streams of water.

Joe stayed back and ran the valves at the engine. "That's everything, Cap. I'm maxing you out on the two and a half."

"Roger that," acknowledged the captain. He keyed his radio. "Maintaining deluge."

There wasn't much for Rex to do on this job. The fire was contained to the floating barge and no one was on board. It didn't matter, though. Rex couldn't think of any place he'd rather be.

As Rex moved closer to the bank, he spotted some flaming debris fall overboard. The huge hunks of refuse didn't submerge, so they stayed alight. However, no longer tethered to the barge, they began to float downriver — heading straight for a group of gasoline storage tanks.

Rex pointed his snout at the debris and barked as loudly as possible. Sparky, Green Point's mascot and now Rex's good friend, spotted it as well. She joined Rex and added her bark to his.

Connor ran up to the dog. He turned back to his team. "Hit that flare up!" he ordered. "Straight stream!"

Holding the powerful hose, Pep and Terence shuffled to the side. They angled their stream toward the flaming trash. Within moments, it was extinguished.

Connor remained near the dogs as the barge fire was beaten back. It was only a matter of time before it was out completely. Rex turned to Sparky and wagged his tail. Sparky wagged hers as well. Then she gave his nose a gentle lap. Yes, Rex wouldn't want to be anywhere else.

Jessie Presley ran up to Connor. She held out her cell phone. "It's my daughter." She gave Connor the phone. "You better hear this yourself."

The captain held the phone to his ear. "Go ahead, JJ."

Rex cocked his head, straining to listen through the roar of the flames behind him. His keen hearing picked up JJ's voice talking, but all he could make out were bits and pieces. One thing was for sure, Shane was in trouble. He looked at Jessie's worried expression, then at Connor's wrinkled brow. He turned and stared back toward the city. A small orange glow hovered above the buildings a few blocks away. The glow came from a part of the city Rex knew extremely well.

Rex didn't wait for the others. He barked and sprinted down the dark street. He ran as fast as his four paws could carry him. He ran straight for Dogpatch.

25

The glow in the night sky grew as Rex ran closer to the station. As he turned the last corner, his fear was realized: Dogpatch Station was in flames. Smoke billowed from the roof as fire lapped out of the two front windows. He poured on the speed.

As he got closer, he realized he didn't know how he was going to get inside. The large bay doors were shut and the smaller entry door was undoubtedly locked. He turned toward the smaller door anyway. With any luck, he could dive through its glass panel. It wasn't breakaway stunt glass, but if he ran fast enough, he thought he could break through. Luckily, he didn't have to.

The door swung open, and Zack Hayden stepped

outside. What was he doing there? The dog knew he had to be up to no good. Hayden wouldn't be making his escape if he were there for legitimate reasons. Rex planted his paws in front of the man and growled.

Hayden halted, startled. "Whoa-whoa!" He backed through the doorway. "Nice doggie. Nice doggie!"

Rex drove him back into the main bay. Flames spread across the high ceiling, and smoke choked the air. Shane was in there somewhere.

Hayden grabbed a nearby turnout coat and swung it at Rex. "Back, mutt! Back!"

The dog ducked the coat on the first swing. On the second, he caught a sleeve in his mouth. Rex shook his head violently, wrenching the coat from the man's hands. He tossed it aside and viciously barked at Hayden, stalking ever closer.

The city manager made a dash for the old phone booth. He slipped inside and closed the door just as Rex slammed against it. Rex barked in frustration. He took two steps back, then flung himself against the glass door a second time. It didn't give.

143

Rex would have to leave the man be. Shane was somewhere in the burning fire station. He left Hayden and ran toward the back. Yet, as he closed in, a burning beam fell from above, blocking his advance. Rex whimpered in frustration. There was no way to get to the entire back half of the station.

Then he figured it out. Rex ran across the bay and galloped up the stairs. He dashed through the bullpen and into the dorm. The back wall seethed with flames. Rex could feel his hair beginning to singe with every step. But he had to make it to one thing in that room — the fire pole.

As he inched closer, he craned his neck to peer into the hole. He saw the coast was clear. Rex shifted his gaze back up to the fire pole. He was trained to climb ladders, walk the thinnest tight-ropes, and even jump from several stories into a stunt bag. He wasn't, however, trained to slide down a pole. Even during his time at Dogpatch, he'd been too frightened to try it.

The dog took a few steps back and crouched. It was now or never. He ran deep into the burning room and leapt into the air. When his stomach

144

slammed into the pole, he shut his eyes and wrapped all four legs around it. He held on tightly as he quickly slid to the first floor. The dog slammed to the ground. When he was sure it was over, he slowly opened his eyes. He had a very sore rear end, but he was alive.

Rex scrambled to his feet and ran into the mess hall. Shane lay unconscious on the floor. Rex licked all over his face, doing the best to revive him.

Finally, Shane stirred. He opened his eyes and smiled. "Dewey." Rex panted happily and wagged his tail as hard as he could.

Using Rex to brace himself, Shane slowly got to his feet. "Let's get out of here, boy," he said.

Rex led the way back toward the bay. Then more of the ceiling collapsed, slamming shut the mess hall door. They ran back to the kitchen, jumped over flaming debris, and made for the kitchen's back door. Shane slammed into it. It didn't budge. They were trapped.

26

Connor watched in horror as they pulled up to the burning firehouse. He no longer cared about the building itself. With a fire this big, there was no way to save it completely. All they could do now was to douse it as best they could and keep it from spreading. What horrified Connor Fahey the most was that JJ told him Shane was inside.

He leapt from the cab before the truck rolled to a stop. "Shane!" he yelled over the rumbling flames.

He ran to the front door. As he reached for the handle, he felt arms wrap around his waist. "Watch it, Cap!" said Terence as he flung him to one side.

The glass exploded and flames shot through the window.

As Joe and Lionel pulled out the hoses, Pep and Terence began to hack at one of the bay doors with their axes. Connor checked his oxygen tank and mask. He was going in after his son.

When a big enough hole was cut away, Connor charged toward it. To his surprise, Zack Hayden stumbled through.

"Zack?" Connor grabbed the man by the shoulders. "Where's Shane?"

"I don't know," he replied. The man doubled over and coughed. "The place was in flames when I arrived. I thought I heard someone inside . . . but I couldn't find him. I tried. . . . I really did."

Connor ushered him toward the others. "Get him oxygen," he ordered. "But don't let him leave." Connor plunged through the splintered hole and into the inferno.

Fire was everywhere. The upstairs was completely engulfed, and the opposite end of the bay wasn't far behind. The wall to the mess hall burned and the smoke was so thick he could hardly see. Connor knew the place was about to come down on top of him. He didn't know if he could even find Shane.

Then, through the thundering noise, he heard a dog barking.

"Shane!" yelled Connor.

"Dad!" came a distant voice. "In here!"

Connor ran toward the mess hall, the only place anyone could survive. He leapt over a burning beam and darted to the door. He looked through the small window. Shane and Dewey were huddled inside. The kitchen beyond them was in flames, but the mess hall was just beginning to catch. Although the room was thick with smoke, they were safe for now.

"Are you okay?" Connor yelled.

Shane coughed. "It's hard to breathe."

Connor tried to open the metal door. It was jammed. "Get back and stay low!" he yelled. He swung the ax and slammed it against the door. It barely moved. He swung again and again. The door didn't budge and he had only three thin dents to show for it.

Shane poked his head up to the window. "The hinges!" Shane pointed down. "I need your ax!"

"If I break this window, that fire is going to flash!" yelled Connor.

"Trust me, Dad!" shouted Shane.

Connor knew that once the window broke, more oxygen would be sucked into the room. The flames would be fed and the fire would flash around them. He also knew that they had no other choice.

Connor shattered the glass with his ax and watched as the kitchen flames grew with new life. They reached toward his son like fiery fingers of a giant hand. Dewey barked a warning.

He passed the ax through. "Hurry, Shane!" he yelled. Then he watched as the boy slammed the ax against the hinges. The bottom one broke with one swing, but the top one took three hits.

"Got it!" yelled Shane.

"Stand back!" yelled Connor. He slammed his shoulder against the door. It fell into the mess hall.

Shane dropped the ax as Connor embraced him. He jerked the boy over the fallen door and into the bay. Dewey scrambled after them.

Connor turned to leave but couldn't see the hole they cut through the bay door. Smoke enveloped everything. He reached down and found Dewey's collar. "Get us out of here, Dewey." The dog barked and led the three of them across the bay toward the thin gash of light.

Once they were outside, Connor helped Shane stagger to the fire truck. Pep placed an oxygen mask over Shane's face as Connor pulled his off. He was about to rejoin his team when Shane grabbed his arm.

"Wait," said Shane. "Where's Zack Hayden?"

"Just relax," said Connor.

Shane shook his head. "No, he set the fires, Dad. All of them. Even set the mill fire."

Fury boiled inside of Connor. He marched to the back of the emergency truck and found Lionel giving oxygen to Hayden. The city manager's eyes widened with fear.

"Is it true?" asked Connor. He ripped the mask from the man's face. "Is it true?"

"No one was supposed to get hurt," Hayden explained.

Connor grabbed the man's coat with both hands. As he pulled him to his feet, Terence and Lionel grabbed the captain's shoulders. "What about my brother?" Hayden struggled to break free, but Connor held tight. "You were a firefighter!" he roared. "What about my son?"

Hayden wrenched free from Connor's grasp. He tried to run but was stopped cold by Pep's fist. Zack Hayden crumpled to the ground, out cold. "Whoops," said Pep. "My bad."

As Lionel and Terence moved in to pick up Hayden, Connor went back to his son. He sat beside him and put an arm around his shoulders. Dewey lay down at their feet. The three of them watched as the Dogpatch team finished extinguishing their own station.

Finally, Connor smiled at his son. "You were pretty cool in there."

Shane wrapped an arm around his dad's waist. "Must be in my DNA."

27

Shane looked out at the large crowd that gathered around City Hall. He stood on the top of the steps next to his dad, the Dogpatch team, and Dewey. Shane wore his best suit, and the team all wore their dress uniforms. Shane felt very proud.

The mayor retold the story of how Shane and Dewey had uncovered Corbin Sellars's plan and how they caught *former* city manager Zack Hayden red-handed. He went on to award medals to the entire team and special medals of commendation to Shane and Dewey. When the mayor draped the medal around the dog's neck, everyone laughed as Dewey extended a paw for the mayor to shake.

As Shane and the team posed for photographs, he looked out at the smiling faces. When he saw Trey Falcon and Liz Knowles, his elation fizzled away. He knew Dewey would have to leave right after the ceremony.

When most of the spectators had finally cleared away, Shane watched as reporters crowded around Trey, Liz, and Dewey. They asked questions about past movies, current love-interest rumors, and other things that Shane didn't think were very important.

"Trey," said one reporter, shoving his microphone in Trey's face. "Can you confirm Rex will make his Broadway debut in *The Canine Mutiny*?"

"He's been approached," replied Trey.

There was a tap on Shane's shoulder. "Hey, Shane," said JJ. "Cool medal."

Shane looked down at the silver medal hanging from his neck. "Yeah, it's all right, I guess." He turned it over in his hand.

"So . . ." said JJ, "my mom was wondering if you and your dad wanted to go get ice cream with us?"

"Me and my dad?" That grabbed his attention. He looked at her and smiled. "Um . . . sure. He'd probably like that. Yeah."

JJ smiled back and went to join the others.

Shane's dad appeared at his side. "Time to say good-bye, chief." He pointed to Dewey.

After the reporters had dwindled away, Shane and his dad walked up to Trey, Liz, and Dewey. Shane stooped beside the terrier. "I know your real name is Rex. . . ." The dog wagged his tail. "But you'll always be Dewey to me." Shane wrapped his arms around him and hugged him tightly. "I'll come visit you real soon."

"I don't think so, Shane," said Trey.

"Trey!" snapped Liz.

"You promised him," pleaded Connor.

"I changed my mind," said Trey. Before Shane could protest, the man offered the end of the leash. "After being a real hero, he'd never be happy just acting like one."

Speechless, Shane stood and took the leash

from the man. After letting go, it was Trey's turn to hug the dog. "So long, Wonder Dog."

Shane and his dad watched as Trey and Liz climbed into their limo and drove away. Dewey barked a good-bye, then looked up at the boy. He wagged his tail and happily panted.

28

Dewey trotted down the stairs of the newly rebuilt Dogpatch Station. Their first day back, the entire team helped move in equipment. The dog quickly scampered out of the way as Terence slowly carried in a large box. The young man slipped and almost dropped it.

Holding a new electric mixer, Joe shook his head as he walked by. "Easy, rookie," he said. "That's my new bun warmer!"

Lionel came down the stairs just as Pep pried open a large wooden crate. A brand-new engine sat before them.

Lionel held his hands over his eyes. "My eyes," he shouted. "It's so bright and . . . clean."

Pep laughed. "I love your kids, Lionel. But this is the baby I've been waiting for."

The telephone rang and everyone scrambled for the wall phone.

"I got it," shouted Lionel.

"Too late," yelled Pep, cutting in front of him.

"I'm closest," said Terence, reaching for the phone.

"I'm biggest," said Joe. He jerked the phone away from Terence and held it to his ear. "Dogpatch. Proud home of Engine Fifty-five. May I help you?"

Dewey trotted to the back of the bay. There, he saw Shane hanging framed replacement photos on the unit's Wall of Honor. All the old ones took their same positions. Then Shane hung a new photo on the wall. It was a picture of Dewey. A tag beneath it read DEWEY, DOGPATCH MASCOT.

Dewey wagged his tail as Shane hung it beside the others. Then Shane laughed as Dewey reached up and straightened it with his paw.

Suddenly, the alarm sounded.

Connor slid down the pole. "Let's go, Dogpatch!" He ran to join the others at their rows of uniforms.

The team got dressed in record time. Connor

checked his watch as they ran to the engine. "Suit-up in fifty seconds!" he announced. The team cheered as they climbed aboard the rig.

Shane patted Dewey on the head. "Go get 'em, boy!"

As the truck pulled out of the bay, Dewey took off after it. He ran alongside, then leapt into Connor's open passenger door. The siren wailed and Dewey hung his head out the window. With his ears and tongue flapping in the breeze, he knew this was where he was meant to be. He was a real hero. He was a firehouse dog!